A faint che street.

Nick watched and stepped out. H.... ... was pulled back in a high ponytail, waving in the breeze like a red flag, and every ounce of testosterone in his body was urging him to charge.

Their eyes met and the impact hit hard— a swift kick of desire straight to his gut. Just the sight of her sent him back to that moment in her kitchen. A moment he still couldn't decide had really happened or not. But he did know one thing for sure: he should have kissed her. If he had, he wouldn't be wondering now.... He'd *know*.

For a brief moment he'd forgotten about his daughter beside him...and the tangled mess of the Clearville grapevine. Darcy had that effect on him. So what if, for a split second, he wasn't a single dad, worried and scarred? With Darcy, he was something else. A man interested in a woman....

Dear Reader,

Have you ever had the chance to start over? The phrase sounds so hopeful, doesn't it? A clean slate, the possibility of a new beginning… The reality of a fresh start can be challenging, though. How do you get over the mistakes of the past and overcome the fear of repeating them?

For Darcy Dawson, a new start means a move to a small town and an opportunity for a new business. But a new love with the town's serious—and seriously handsome— veterinarian is the last thing on her mind.

Nick Pirelli thinks he's ready for a new relationship with the right kind of woman, but will painful lessons from the past keep him from opening his heart to a city girl like Darcy?

Darcy and the Single Dad is the first book in my new Special Edition miniseries, The Pirelli Brothers. I hope you enjoy it. Look for Sam's and Drew's stories in the future!

Happy reading!

Stacy Connelly

DARCY AND THE SINGLE DAD

STACY CONNELLY

HARLEQUIN®
entertain, enrich, inspire™

Recycling programs
for this product may
not exist in your area.

ISBN-13: 978-0-373-65719-3

DARCY AND THE SINGLE DAD

Books by Stacy Connelly

Harlequin Special Edition

Her Fill-In Fiancé #2128
Temporary Boss...Forever Husband #2148
*Darcy and the Single Dad #2237

Silhouette Special Edition

All She Wants for Christmas #1944
Once Upon a Wedding #1992
The Wedding She Always Wanted #2033

*The Pirelli Brothers

Other books by Stacy Connelly available in ebook format.

STACY CONNELLY

has dreamed of publishing books since she was a kid, writing stories about a girl and her horse. Eventually, boys made it onto the page as she discovered a love of romance and the promise of happily ever after.

When she is not lost in the land of make-believe, Stacy lives in Arizona with her two spoiled dogs. She loves to hear from readers and can be contacted at stacyconnelly@cox.net or www.stacyconnelly.com.

To Gail Chasan and Susan Litman—

Thank you for this chance at my first series
for Special Edition. I'm looking forward to
telling all the Pirelli brothers' stories!

Chapter One

Nick Pirelli was exhausted. Staring out the windshield of his SUV, he was glad he knew the back routes around his hometown as well as he did. The evergreen-lined asphalt curving through the mountains had landed more than one tourist—and the occasional local—in a ditch or with a new guard-rail-shaped hood ornament. But even under the dark skies of an approaching storm, he could easily find his way.

It had been one hell of a day. Nick had worked as Clearville, California's only vet for years, and most days, he loved his job. He had an affinity for animals and recognized the joy they brought to people's lives with their loyalty and affection. In his almost ten years as a vet, he'd learned to control his emotions to best deal with the animals and owners who trusted him with their care. He'd treated injuries and accidents and the heartbreak of old age.

But the horse the sheriff had called him out to evaluate wasn't sick or injured or old.

Instead, it had been abandoned and left to fend for itself in a weed-and-debris-filled paddock. Nick didn't know how people could walk away from someone who depended on them. Who needed them.

The animal had stood still as Nick and the sheriff debated its fate, head bowed, posture as poor as the pitiful creature had to feel. But in that moment of decision, the horse's head rose and it looked right at Nick. Its eyes had been dull and listless, but in the soulful brown gaze, he saw a hint of... It was ridiculous to call it hope in such a hopeless situation, but he'd seen a flicker of something. Maybe just the ghost of a chance that with a little care, a little love, the future could be so much brighter.

Not wanting to look too closely at the reason why the horse's plight seemed to reach inside and grab hold of his gut, he'd pulled out his phone. Within the hour, Jarrett Deeks had arrived with a trailer hitched to his king cabin truck.

None of the local rescues would have the resources or ability to even try to nurse a horse this far gone back to health.

The horse barely had the strength to walk, but the two of them managed to ease it into the trailer. Nick had followed Jarrett out to his property. He gave the former rodeo star all the instructions he could, promising to check on the horse the next day and letting Jarrett know he could call for help at any time.

Nick was still wondering if he'd made the right choice as he headed home. Only time would tell. For now, he was looking forward to relaxing and, hopefully, leaving this day behind. With nothing more pressing to do, he planned to spend a few hours in front of the television, enjoying a baseball game and having a beer. Alone.

Thanks to a slumber party his daughter, Maddie, had

been invited to, he had a weekend to himself, and he was looking forward to it with enough anticipation to send guilt dogging his heels.

After all, Maddie had just gotten back from a trip to San Francisco to see her mother. He shouldn't have wanted—needed—a break so soon. The only saving grace was that Maddie had missed her friends during her two weeks away and had been thrilled with the invitation to stay with the Martins.

So, really, he had no reason to feel guilty at all.

Trying to force the feeling aside, he focused on the cold, crisp taste of the beer waiting for him at home, the smoky flavor of the burgers he'd cook on the charcoal grill, the peace and quiet of having the house to himself. The cabin in the woods he and his younger brother Drew had built together was more than a home to Nick. It was his haven, his sanctuary, his—

Cave.

He'd heard the gibe from more than one family member, and he was tired of listening to their complaints that he was turning into a hermit. Hell, some days he was tired of *being* a hermit, a realization that had blindsided him more than once lately. The most recent blow had been at his parents' anniversary party a few weeks ago, a celebration concluding with his sister Sophia's engagement to Jake Cameron.

The newly engaged couple had glowed, lit from within by their emotions for each other. His little sister deserved that kind of happiness and a man who loved her as completely and utterly as Jake did. Already they'd worked their way through some daunting hurdles with Jake having to earn Sophia's trust after she'd been betrayed by a man she'd met before Jake. A man who was the biological father to the baby Sophia carried. But Jake had already vowed to love the baby as much as he loved its mother, and no one in the Pirelli family doubted his word.

Love—strong and solid after his parents' thirty-five years of marriage and as bright and shiny as the engagement ring his sister now wore—had surrounded him and yet Nick had somehow felt apart from it all. His mother's words had only multiplied the feeling of life and love passing him by as she'd embraced his sister in a tearful hug. "I can't believe my little girl is getting married! It seems like only yesterday you were Maddie's age."

Nick had immediately looked toward Maddie, his own little girl who he feared was ready to make her eight-going-on-eighteen leap in a blink of his eye.

His hands tightened on the wheel. This last trip to San Francisco over summer vacation—or more specifically, Maddie's return from that vacation—solidified Nick's fears.

His daughter was changing.

At first, after Christmas and then spring break, he'd convinced himself the changes were merely superficial. The new outfits that cost more than his entire wardrobe combined. The haircut too sophisticated for an eight-year-old. Underneath it all, he'd told himself, Maddie was still his Maddie. His little girl.

But this time, he couldn't close his eyes to what was happening. His concerns had hardened into cement blocks around his ankles, and no matter how he struggled, he felt himself going under. Getting in over his head while Maddie drifted further and further away. Because each time his daughter left their small hometown of Clearville to visit her mother, she came back…different. A little less the girl he knew and a little more the woman he'd married.

But a girl needed her mother, so he'd done his best to accommodate Carol's requests to see their daughter even after she'd walked out on both of them with little warning five years earlier.

Lately, the uneasy feeling that his ex wanted more time with Maddie had crept into his gut whenever they spoke. Not that Carol had come out and said anything directly, but then that wasn't her style. She was more subtle and sly. Like the most recent visit when Carol had sadly informed Maddie they had time to go to SeaWorld or Disneyland but couldn't possibly do both.

Nick had known extending the trip would be playing right into Carol's hands, and he'd been damn close to telling her she could take Maddie to SeaWorld and *he'd* take her to Disneyland. But one thought stopped him. He didn't want to take Maddie only to have her wishing the whole time her mother was the one holding her hand through the happiest place on earth.

Nick was glad his daughter enjoyed her visits with her mother. If Maddie was happy, he was happy. Most of the time, he could even convince himself it was true; after all, it wasn't Maddie's happiness that worried him. It was how unhappy she was when she returned that had his gut tangled in knots.

He'd hoped his sister Sophia's upcoming wedding and Maddie's role as flower girl would give her something to look forward to, but she wasn't nearly as excited as he'd expected. He couldn't figure it out. With her recent fascination of all things girly, he'd thought she'd jump at the chance to be in the wedding party. He just didn't get little girls.

Nick snorted. Hell, it wasn't like he got women, either.

Maybe that was what happened when a man was single for too long.

His jaw tightened, and he half expected a lightning bolt from the approaching storm to strike him down. Hadn't he said it'd be a cold day before he *ever* took a chance on another relationship?

But watching Sophia and Jake together, he'd envied their courage to risk heartbreak for the reward of finding love again. He felt as though something had hit him in the chest in that moment, striking the emptiness inside him like a blow to a bass drum. Even now, weeks later, the reverberations still vibrated inside him, urging him to...do something.

But Nick wasn't a man to give into rash impulses. He'd learned his lesson after trying to turn a heated, whirlwind affair into a long-term relationship. If that hadn't already made him cautious, he also had Maddie to consider. Word of his first date would spread throughout town before he'd glanced at the dinner menu, and the woman would likely have nieces or nephews—if not a son or daughter—who went to school with Maddie.

The idea of putting his daughter through that kind of speculation—of putting himself through it—had kept at bay any thoughts of trying to date as a single dad. Until now....

The buzz of Nick's cell interrupted his thoughts. A glance at the screen showed his office number, and he cringed. If Jarrett Deeks was having trouble with the horse, he'd have called him directly, so Nick could only hope that whatever his assistant needed could wait until tomorrow.

Answering the call on speaker, he said, "I'm on my way home, Rhonda. Unless this is an emergency—"

"Oh, but it is," the forty-something woman replied with a hint of amusement in her voice.

The first splatter of rain hit the windshield, and Nick bit back a curse. "If this is some kind of a joke—"

"Hey, don't shoot the messenger, Doc."

Nick sighed, mentally kissing his beer and ball game goodbye. "What's the emergency?"

"Darcy Dawson called. She said she 'needs the doctor right away.'"

Personal experience reminded him Darcy Dawson's voice sounded nothing like his assistant's pack-a-day rasp. Darcy had a just-out-of-bed-sexy murmur and a laugh that stroked like fingernails down a man's spine.

"Better watch out," Rhonda was warning him with a fair share of teasing in her tone. "I'm surprised Darcy hasn't tried making a play for you or one of your brothers already. The three Pirelli boys are some of the best catches in town. You're all young, successful, single—"

"Give me a break, Rhonda," Nick said with a snort of laughter at his assistant's joking and the implication that he, like his brothers, was free to have the kind of fling Darcy Dawson had become known for in her less than two months in Clearville. He had Maddie to think about, and even though she was still a little girl, he was painfully aware how the decisions he made could affect her.

Doubly aware, he felt, since Carol wasn't always as discriminating as he thought she should be. He'd made it more than plain to his ex-wife a few years ago— when Maddie came home talking about the "sleepovers" her mother had—that he didn't want any of Carol's casual boyfriends around his daughter.

Carol had turned his words back on him, insisting he, too, keep his girlfriends away from Maddie, and Nick had immediately agreed. He hadn't known any women in Clearville he'd want to have a casual fling with then.

You still don't know any, he mentally berated a libido that had taken immediate notice the very first time he heard Darcy Dawson's laugh.

He'd been standing one row over at the grocery store,

trying fruitlessly to decide on the hair bands his daughter had sent him to the store to buy. But the moment he'd heard that laugh, he'd forgotten all about them. Heaven help him, for a moment he'd forgotten all about being a single father, and before he knew where he was going, he'd sought out the woman behind that laugh.

Fortunately within the first glance, he'd come back to his senses. Well, mostly, since he hadn't been able to get Darcy Dawson out of his mind since. Still, it had only taken that first look to know Darcy wasn't the kind of woman he was looking for. Wasn't the kind of woman a man ever *found,* not in Clearville, at least.

A pair of expensive oversize sunglasses propped on the top of her head held back a tumble of shoulder-length red hair and she carried a purse that likely cost more than the monthly payment on his SUV. Her clothes—a tailored white shirt belted over narrow black trousers that hugged a pair of legs that seemed to go on forever before ending in spiky heels—spoke of a fashionable, sophisticated woman. Not the kind he was looking for, he'd determined, and that was before he'd learned of her reputation.

Single or not, he didn't have the freedom his younger brothers did. Sam especially enjoyed the opportunity to have a good time. He'd dive into a fling with Darcy Dawson headfirst and come out smelling like roses on the other side. Women could never stay angry at Sam.

Normally, *Nick* could never stay angry at Sam, but just the thought of his youngest brother and Darcy Dawson together made his jaw clench tight enough to crack.

"Did Ms. Dawson say what the emergency is?"

"Nope. Her cell phone started breaking up before she could say. Funny thing, I didn't even know she had any pets."

Deciding he was having some cell problems of his own, Nick hung up on his assistant's chortling laugh.

Having his name even temporarily linked with Darcy Dawson's would only scare off the right kind of woman. His ill-fated marriage to Carol was already something of a black mark against him. He didn't need to be down two strikes before he even came up to bat.

Maddie needed a positive female influence. Sure, his mother had been around her entire life, and Sophia had recently moved back to town, but a grandmother and aunt weren't the same as a mother. Someone who could be a constant, consistent, solid presence in Maddie's life. Someone who was small town, with Clearville roots dug deep in her soul. That was the kind of woman Nick was looking for.

This time, he was going to be damn sure he made the right choice from the start. He couldn't risk jumping on and off some kind of dating-go-round, asking out any woman who happened to spin by. His failed marriage and Carol's desertion had made him cautious, but Nick knew once he found the right woman, he'd have to jump in with both feet, hang on and not let go. Because try as he might, after looking at the idea from every angle—up, down, inside and out—he couldn't work his way around one simple fact.

If Maddie needed a mother, then he needed a wife. Because God help him, he couldn't figure out how to get one without the other.

The dog hadn't moved.

Crouched down at the back stairs, Darcy Dawson squinted toward the far side of the crawl space beneath the porch. Every now and then, in the flashes of lightning that lit the darkness, she could see the reflection from the dog's eyes, her only indication the animal was still there.

Worry trickled through her, and she shivered, pulling up the collar of her coat closer around her ears.

She'd tried using the lure of the kibble, but the dog refused to come out of hiding. Refused, too, to eat from the bowl Darcy had shoved as far as she dared in the cramped space. She might have blamed fear of the storm for the dog's behavior except it had holed up before the lightning and rain had begun.

Even though Darcy didn't know anything about dogs, she knew something was wrong. But she didn't know what it was or what she could do to offer any comfort.

Helplessness rose up inside her. "It's just a dog," she muttered against the lump in her throat. "You don't even like dogs."

The words echoing through her thoughts for the past half hour were a lie, and saying them out loud didn't help convince Darcy they were true. She didn't *dislike* dogs, but she was afraid of them. Had been since she'd been bitten by a neighbor's dog when she was little.

Her fingers slipped past the collar of her sweater and she traced the scars along her shoulder, reminders from that long-ago day. As a kid, she'd shied away from dogs, and as an adult living in an apartment in Portland, she hadn't been around them much. She simply didn't go places where dogs were likely to be, and if she saw one in passing... Well, she just passed quickly.

But her move to the small town of Clearville, California, was supposed to be about making a new start and living in the moment. So when a stray dog wandered into her backyard after she'd left open the gate, she decided that maybe it was time to put her fear of dogs in the past, as well. Not that she planned to *keep* the dog; she wasn't that certain of her ability to let go of a twenty-year-old phobia, but something in the animal's crouched, uncertain posture spoke to her.

And, she had to admit, the dog was…interesting. A mix of silver and black from its alert ears down to its tail with brown and white spots on its face and legs. And its eyes—one brown and one blue—fascinated Darcy with their watchful intelligence. Of course, she'd only noticed thanks to the zoom feature on her digital camera. She hadn't actually gotten near enough to see the dog's two-toned eyes up close.

But she printed the pictures she'd taken, placing "Found Dog" posters around town. She'd also bought a bag of dog food and some toys at the grocery store and folded up an old comforter for a bed in the sheltered corner of the porch. None of which nominated her for Pet Parent of the Year, but just knowing the dog was in her backyard pushed Darcy out of her comfort zone.

Still, she'd been certain, in a town the size of Clearville, the owner would come forward in no time. Or that someone would recognize such a unique dog and know who it belonged to. She'd even imagined the scene —reuniting the poor lost dog with its grateful, tearful owners. Darcy would wave off their praise and offer of a reward, content to see owner and pet back together again.

But after a week, no one had called, and Darcy had started to wonder what she would do if the dog's owner never showed.

Sometimes facing your fears is the only way to escape them. Her mother's encouragement rang in her head, strong and sure.

But then her mother had always been brave.

The ache wasn't as sharp as it had been following her mother's death a year ago, but time had done little to lessen Darcy's sense of loss. She blinked back tears. Her voice was rough around the lump in her throat as she whispered, "You always did say we should get a dog."

Alanna had raised Darcy to be confident, strong, proud. Lessons Darcy tried to live by, but ones she'd failed recently. She'd been devastated by her mother's death. Feeling so alone, she'd reached out blindly to grab hold of the first lifeline she could find. But Aaron Utley hadn't helped her out of her misery as much as he'd taken advantage of it.

It was the only explanation Darcy had for falling so hard and so fast.

He'd seemed so charming and caring, Darcy somehow missed when that care transformed into control as he tried to mold her into the perfect accessory for an up-and-coming lawyer.

And she'd foolishly gone along. Hoping to ease the ache of sorrow and emptiness, she had convinced herself she was in love. For months, she poured her heart and soul into trying to be the perfect girlfriend and then the perfect fiancée. Only after gaining distance from Aaron had Darcy realized how fully he'd manipulated her. How he'd used her as his emotional punching bag, constantly setting her up simply to knock her down.

Thank God she'd gotten out before trying to be the perfect wife! She didn't need anyone to tell her what a failure she would have been as Mrs. Aaron Utley.

But the anger following their breakup had been the kick in the butt Darcy needed to put aside her sorrow and recall the wonderful times she'd had with her mother. It had always been just the two of them, and they'd shared everything. Including her mother's dream of moving back to the tiny Northern California town where she'd been raised and opening a small beauty boutique on Main Street.

Alanna wanted to take the knowledge she'd gained from her years managing a dozen different locations of a major department store chain and focus it on her own business. Moving then opening the shop had always been planned for a distant "someday," but her death had taught Darcy to take advantage of today, and she was determined to make her mother's dream a reality.

She refused to consider what she would do if she failed, so she'd handled it all—moving to a town where she didn't know a soul, renting a century-old house in need of serious updating and planning a grand opening for a new business at a time when many shops were closing. If she had any doubts, any worries, she'd keep them hidden behind a confident facade where no one would see.

Fake it 'til you make it, her mother would say.

The wind shifted again, sending rain pelting against her back and running in icy rivulets down the collar of her coat. Another spark of lightning briefly illuminated the sky, but it was long enough for Darcy to see the dog lying on its side, its watchful gaze still focused on her.

"And we are going to make it," she said as another clap of thunder rattled the house. "The vet's coming, and he'll make everything okay."

After the agonizing days she'd spent in the hospital at her mother's side, Darcy was painfully aware sometimes even the best doctors couldn't help. But what she knew in her head didn't change what she felt in her heart. She may have only met Nick Pirelli in passing, but the vet exuded confidence and control Darcy envied. He wouldn't be stuck in the rain at a loss, not knowing what to do or what to say. He was the type to push those kinds of people aside and take over and do what needed to be done.

A low rumble sounded from the front of the house. At first, Darcy thought it was another distant roll of thunder until she heard a vehicle door slam. "He's here," she whispered to the dog. "He'll make everything all right."

Pushing up from the muddy ground, Darcy felt her heart pound in her chest as she lowered her head against the rain and ducked beneath the shelter of the wide eaves on her Craftsman-style house. She was worried about the dog, afraid Nick Pirelli might confirm her fears that the animal was sick. It was enough to make any compassionate person's pulse quicken, knees weaken, breath catch.

Who was she trying to kid? She'd felt that same quickening, weakening, catching sensation when she had first laid eyes on Nick Pirelli in the town's grocery.

He was tall, over six feet, with intense, solemn brown eyes and dark, thick hair. Darcy could tell in that first glance that Nick Pirelli wasn't a man given to spending much time on his appearance, and why should he when he was as close to masculine perfection as she'd seen? But she could also tell that what time he did spend in front of the mirror was used to try to tame the hint of natural wave in his mahogany hair into some kind of order.

Darcy didn't know why that had struck her as so endearing, but coupled with the collection of pink and purple head bands he'd been holding, she'd been utterly charmed.

Not that he'd felt the same if his sudden one-eighty and quick disappearance from the aisle where she'd been shopping was anything to go by.

Skirting beneath the dripping eaves as she rounded the front of the house, Darcy ignored the sharp prick of hurt now just as she had then. It didn't matter if Nick Pirelli had listened to all the rumors around town about her or what the too-serious vet thought. He was here to help, to do his job. The only opinion she cared about was a professional one.

But seeing Nick standing on her porch in a beat-up pair of jeans topped by a red and black checked flannel shirt—looking so strong, so sure, so hands-on—Darcy couldn't deny the rush of attraction. One she was determined to ignore. If Nick Pirelli was the type of man to judge her based on a bunch of lies, then she could only imagine what he'd think of her if he knew the truth.

Chapter Two

As Nick lifted his hand to ring Darcy's doorbell, he heard footsteps on the porch behind him. He turned in time to see her rush up the steps toward him. Her dark red hair was caught up in a damp ponytail, and her jacket and jeans were wet. She stopped short, mere inches away, and her feet nearly slipped out from beneath her. Pure reflex had him reaching out to catch her.

And it was reflex that had his hands bracketing her narrow waist, reflex that had him ducking his head to inhale her summery scent, mixed with rain from the storm. Reflex that had him hungering to kiss her, to slide his palms down to her hips, to...

Stay far, far away.

That had been his goal when he'd driven up to her small Craftsman-style cottage at the end of the street. He would be professional and polite—or as polite as he could manage—do his job and get out of there before—before any of *this* could happen.

Jerking away his hands before he could get burned, he stiffly asked, "Are you okay?"

"Yes. Fine. Thanks." The short, choppy response wasn't what he expected. It was almost as if Darcy had been just as affected by the unexpected contact as he had been.

Straightening, she stepped back and wiped her face. Her hair and cheeks were wet from the storm, and her efforts left a streak of mascara beneath one eye. He couldn't imagine why the sight made her seem somehow vulnerable or why it tugged at something inside him, something he hadn't felt in a long, long time.

"Sorry, I don't normally fall over people like this," she said with a wry enough smile to make Nick wonder if she'd heard the gossip in town. Gossip that said falling all over men was *exactly* what she normally did.

Shoving aside thoughts of the rumors, he focused on his reasons for being out in the middle of a storm instead of at home with baseball on the TV and a beer in his hand. "My assistant said you have some kind of emergency." He hoped his voice didn't sound as skeptical to Darcy as it did to him, and figured he must have done a passable job at hiding his doubt when she nodded quickly.

"Yes, and thank you so much—"

"It's okay," he said quickly. "Just doing my job."

"Right. Of course. This way."

After bending down to grab the well-worn, brown leather bag he'd dropped when Darcy had appeared out of nowhere and stumbled into his arms, Nick followed her around to the back of the house. She must have come from that direction, and yet he was a little surprised. Somehow he'd expected her to lead him inside.

Not that he was looking for an invitation. He was just—
He didn't know what he was right then.

And his confusion only increased when Darcy knelt
down before her back porch. The rain had turned the area
to mud, and now that he wasn't so distracted, in the glow
coming through the windows he could see reddish-brown
mud caked the boots she wore and rimmed the hem of her
jeans. She wore a fitted, thigh-length jacket in a rich taupe
color, but her choice had little to do with fashion. Whatever was going on, Darcy had been outside in the storm
for a while.

"...I can't coax her out and she's not eating," Darcy was
saying. "I didn't know what to do."

Squatting down on his heels, Nick got his first look at
the *she* in question. A medium-sized dog lay huddled beneath the porch. "How long has she been like this?"

"Since I came home this afternoon." Darcy crouched
down beside him to peer at the dog. The animal had
crawled through a hole in the rickety latticework framing
the fascia of the porch. A small hole. Small enough that
the two of them were nearly cheek to cheek gazing into it.

Focusing on work instead of giving in to the need to
study Darcy's elegant profile, the arch of her forehead, the
straight slope of her nose, the tempting curve of her lips,
Nick asked, "Has she been out of the yard at all?" An injury might explain the dog's instinctual need to hide. "Or
is there anything she could have gotten into back here?
Pesticides? That kind of thing?"

"No, nothing. But— You think it's something serious
then?"

The worry in her voice called to Nick. He turned toward
the sound, forgetting how close she was. Close enough for
him to be in danger of falling into the endless green of her

eyes. Close enough to be a breath away from feeling her pale pink lips against his....

"I, um—" Nick cleared his throat against the sudden lump of lust lodged there. "I can't tell from here."

He'd learned his lesson when it came to making promises he couldn't keep, but he found himself longing to ease the frown between Darcy's auburn eyebrows.

It's going to be okay. Everything will work out for the best. You'll see.

Those were the vows he'd made to Carol years ago, and he'd failed miserably on all accounts. Nick had never been a man to say he hadn't made mistakes, but he damned sure didn't repeat them.

"Do you have a flashlight?" He needed to try to assess any injuries before moving the dog.

It hadn't been his intention, but somehow his words managed to wring a small smile from Darcy. "Living in this house? I have a flashlight in every room."

He'd heard about the troubles she'd had with the house—faulty electricity, leaky plumbing—typical complaints with a house built at the start of the last century. But it wasn't Darcy's wires or pipes people in town were talking about after she went out with part-time handyman, full-time ladies' man Travis Parker.

No one was surprised when the relationship ended quickly. Travis Parker was known for chasing after a woman only to cut her loose once she was caught. But it was Darcy who kept the rumor mill churning as she seemed willing to give Travis a run for his money as the local heartbreaker, rebounding by going out with two or three other available guys in Clearville.

Not that it was any of his business. Not any of his business at all.

"I'll need a blanket, too," he said abruptly, turning back to the dog and away from Darcy's smile.

He felt the question in her glance as she slowly rose to her feet, but he refused to look her way. He didn't care who Darcy Dawson dated, he told himself as she quickly hurried up the back porch stairs. Her footsteps were light and quick on the creaky porch floorboards, and he wondered how she did that. How she could make something as simple as walking seem like a graceful, rhythmic dance.

Reaching out, Nick grabbed the lattice work with both hands and tugged hard enough to break free more of the weathered wood from the rusty nail heads. The masculine show of force did little to lessen the irritation building inside him. The last thing he needed was to wind up on Darcy Dawson's To Do list. And yeah, okay, the trip wasn't a total goose chase. Darcy really was worried about the dog.

But she'd also really had problems with her wiring and plumbing. That was how things started. Where they ended— Well, Nick didn't let himself think about that. He'd probably tear down the whole porch with his bare hands if he spent too much time imagining Darcy in the arms of those other men.

He needed to concentrate on the job at hand, and after he'd done what he could to help the dog, he'd turn his attention back to his plan for the future. Finding the right kind of woman.

A woman who was responsible and down-to-earth. A woman who walked with her feet firmly on the ground. If she was pretty, he'd consider it a bonus, but certainly not a requirement, Nick decided. He'd allowed his hormones to overrule his head before and, except for Maddie, the results had been disastrous. He didn't need to feel that skip in his heartbeat, that quickening of his pulse, the low throb of desire that hummed beneath the mundane sounds of everyday life.

He knew what he wanted and—

"I've got it."

Darcy's husky voice broke into his thoughts, and Nick could only stare at her. She stood beneath the porch light, so he could see her more clearly now. Even with her thick hair pulled back into a damp ponytail and her makeup mostly washed away by the rain, she was beautiful. Tall and graceful, she definitely had *it*. She was— She was everything he did *not* want in a mother for his child. Everything he didn't want in a wife.

"The flashlight and blanket?" she said, lifting the objects in her arms, her voice hesitant when his silence went on too long.

"Right," he said abruptly. "That's—what I need."

He reached out for the items, careful not to brush his hands against any part of Darcy. Grateful to escape, even though it meant crawling into a muddy hole, Nick ducked beneath the porch and through the space he'd made larger. He half crawled, half slid across the muddy ground.

"Do you need—"

"Just stay back," Nick answered when Darcy's voice followed him into the damp, cramped space. Last thing he needed was for her to try to squeeze in behind him. He'd never been particularly claustrophobic, but the idea of being trapped in such close proximity with the woman had sweat breaking out on his forehead. "I need as much room as I can get in here."

In the glare from the flashlight, the dog eyed him warily. He could see now that she was some kind of heeler mix with a solid, medium-sized build, alert ears and intelligent gaze. He'd always had a soft spot for working-class

dogs, admiring their bravery, their intense watchfulness…
their loyalty.

And after only a quick examination, he was relieved to
discover the reason the dog had sought out some privacy
and shelter. "Come on, girl. Let's find you a more comfortable spot."

He'd asked for the blanket in case she snapped at him
or started to squirm when he moved her. Judging from
her quiet, crouched demeanor, she was clearly afraid, but
Nick didn't sense that fear turning into aggression. He kept
the blanket away from her head as he wrapped her up and
scooted his way back from under the porch.

"What do you think? Is she okay? Are you going to
take her to your clinic?" Darcy's rapid-fire questions were
filled with anxiety, and the dog seemed to shake in time
with each word.

Keeping his voice monotonous and low, Nick wasn't
sure which female he was trying to calm. "She's going to
be fine. All she needs is a clean, dry place to let nature
take its course."

"Nature?" Darcy blinked up at him as he rose to his feet,
and Nick regretted his choice of words. A little too much
nature was already coursing through his body for him to
be saying anything even slightly suggestive.

"She's pregnant," he said.

"Pregnant?" Darcy echoed as she followed him up the
back porch steps. "I didn't— How—"

"That's what happens when owners don't have their
dogs fixed."

"I know that's *how*. But, see the thing is— She's really
not my dog."

A high-pitched squeal interrupted, and they both looked
down at the squeaky rubber toy Nick had stepped on. From
there, Darcy followed his gaze to the bed she'd set up in the

corner of the porch, along with the food and water bowls with their paw-print design, and an array of colorful balls and rawhide bones.

"Okay, so maybe I went a little overboard on my trip to the grocery store, but really, she's not—"

"Not your dog," Nick echoed. "Right."

He'd heard the excuse from owners before. Unwilling to deal with the problems their lack of responsibility caused, they dropped off pregnant dogs and newborn kittens at shelters as "strays."

He tried to help out where he could, working with a shelter in the next town over and volunteering his time with a mobile spay and neuter program. But he'd long ago acknowledged and reluctantly accepted that there were people whose minds he could not change.

Or at least he thought he had. Maybe it was the day he'd had, seeing the horse left to starve by the people entrusted with its care, but he was hit by a wave of disappointment that Darcy was—

What? Not who he thought she was? Not the kind of woman he wanted her to be?

Nick shook off the ridiculous idea. He *didn't* know Darcy and he didn't want to get to know her. She was a city girl who'd quickly tire of playing small-town dress-up and move on when she realized she didn't belong. But for Nick, Clearville was in his blood.

"There's a shelter the next town over." Even in the dim light from the back porch, Nick could see Darcy flinch. A twinge of guilt pricked his conscience for making her feel bad, but he ignored it. He was simply explaining the reality of the situation. "They might have a foster available to take the dog and her pups until they're old enough to be adopted."

Darcy shook her head even as she caught herself raising

her left arm over her chest, reaching for the reminders of the old injury. She stayed the motion when she saw Nick watching her closely. "No. I won't take her to a shelter." Crossing her arms instead, she said, "I—I'll keep her."

The vet arched an eyebrow, his doubt as obvious in the faint lighting as his disbelief had been moments earlier. She could have tried harder to convince him the dog wasn't hers, she supposed. But words could be meaningless, empty things. If he hadn't believed her the first time, why would he the second or third? Darcy refused to argue her innocence with someone who'd predetermined her guilt.

He'd judged her and found her lacking. Well, so what? She had nothing to prove to him. She had nothing to prove to anyone but herself.

Nick Pirelli could believe what he wanted. She didn't care. Or at least she wouldn't…as soon as she convinced herself that was true.

"You really think you can handle this?"

With the dog cradled in his arms, Nick never raised his voice above that low murmur she'd heard coming from beneath the porch. A sound that, at that time, had washed over her and soothed away her worry. It hadn't even mattered that he'd been talking to the dog. That mellow, hypnotic baritone would have had her willingly climbing into his arms.

Now, with the same tone of voice doing little to disguise his doubt, Darcy's cheeks started to heat. Her instant attraction to the dark-haired vet was as unexpected as it was embarrassing considering his own less-than-flattering opinion of her. But she had bigger things to worry about at the moment. Or rather several little things.…

"I'll have to handle it, won't I? Wait… Where are you going?" she asked when Nick awkwardly reached with one hand for the screen door while still carrying the dog wrapped in the blanket.

For a split second, she thought she saw something soften in Nick's expression, but then his gaze dropped to the dog in his arms. When he looked up again, his dark look was remote. "She needs to be someplace dry and warm and quiet. Someplace *inside*."

Inside? She was going to have— Her mind blanked at the sheer number of potential dogs inside her house.

"Where do you want me to put her?"

For a brief moment, Darcy panicked. She wouldn't take the dog to a shelter, but Nick was a vet. Surely he could find someplace else. But then she looked at the poor dog who seemed to be quietly waiting for her decision, and she couldn't do it. She couldn't turn her back now.

"There's a laundry room right off the kitchen." Other than housing her washer and dryer and storing products for her boutique until she was ready to open, the laundry room was empty. Darcy led the way through the country-style kitchen and into the other space.

Hurriedly, she tried to scoop up the bras and panties she'd left folded on top of the dryer. Heat flooded her face, though she didn't know why. Nick Pirelli wasn't the least bit interested in her or her underwear. After stuffing the pieces of lace and satin back into the dirty clothes hamper, she pushed some boxes out of the way.

"I'll go—" Her words cut off as she tried scooting around Nick to head back to the patio for the dog's blanket and bowls. The laundry room that had seemed plenty spacious before was suddenly too crowded for her to take a single step without bumping into the exasperated vet. And wouldn't you know that the frown on his face didn't take away one iota from his good looks? If anything, the brooding intensity only added to his appeal, making Darcy suddenly understand women who fell for the dark, dangerous hero.

She'd never been the type. Aaron had been an all-American golden boy—blond hair, blue eyes, with an aspiring politician's practiced smile. So different from Nick.

Darcy cut off the pointless comparisons. When Nick inadvertently countered her slide to the right with his own move to the left, she finally grabbed him by the shoulders. Ignoring the sudden flutter in her belly when her hands encountered warm male muscles through the damp softness of his flannel shirt, she led them both in a pirouette that would have done a dance teacher proud.

"I'll be right back with the other blanket and her water bowl. Is there— Should I do anything else?" Darcy asked as she backed out of the room.

Nick knelt down to place the dog on the floor and glanced at her over his broad shoulder. "What? Like boil water?"

"Well, yeah."

"Only if you feel like having some tea."

He turned back to the dog before Darcy had a chance to see his expression. Had Nick Pirelli just told a joke? Darcy almost hoped he hadn't. Grumpy and grouchy, he was hard enough to resist. Throw in a sense of humor, and she might be in some real trouble.

Half an hour later, Nick stepped out of the laundry room and joined Darcy in the kitchen. He shouldn't have been surprised when she held out a steaming mug.

"Chamomile?" she offered, the challenging spark in her green eyes catching his attention and refusing to let go.

For all the talk he'd heard about Darcy Dawson, how was it no one had mentioned her quick wit or her sense of humor? The dangerous combination already had him low-ering his guard and regretting his earlier behavior.

"How's she doing?" Darcy asked with a glance over his shoulder at the narrow doorway.

"She'll be fine." In fact, now was a good time for him to go. Even though the dog was young and likely a first-time mama, nature would tell her what to do. But he hadn't missed Darcy's reaction when he had first told her the dog was having puppies. Her face had gone white, and she'd looked ready to faint. What if Darcy actually did pass out and the dog needed help? Sticking around and making sure the delivery went smoothly was part of his job.

Joining Darcy in the small, intimate kitchen for tea was *not* part of his job, but even as the warning was drifting through his mind, Nick stepped closer and accepted the cup. His jeans were weighted down by mud, clinging un-comfortably to his skin, and his shirt was soaked through, thanks to the rain. It might have been the end of July, but the sudden storm had dropped the temperature, and he took a minute to warm his hands around the mug. "Thanks."

"I should be thanking you. I'm sure you had better things to do than make a house call on a night like tonight."

Nick shrugged. "Comes with the territory."

"So what's it like?" Darcy had stripped off her jacket at some point, revealing a pale green knit sweater that hugged the curves of her breasts, but still wore the dark, wide-legged jeans. Her feet were bare, cherry-red toenails peek-ing out from beneath the mud-splattered hem. He tried not to notice how small and delicate they were, just as he tried not to notice how his own scuffed and scarred size-eleven work boots had tracked mud across the white tile floors.

Darcy leaned back against the butcher block counter, her hands cradling her own mug. Her gaze was open and interested, easily sucking him in until he could barely re-member what she'd even asked. "What's what like?"

"Being a small-town vet?"

Small town. Two simple words that had his hackles standing on end. Yeah, that was what Carol had accused him of being more times than he could count, and the in-sult had hurt. But Carol had been his wife. He'd felt frus-trated and at a loss to keep her happy, and he'd failed her as a husband with his lack of ambition to move to a big city where he could make more money.

Darcy, though, was a stranger, a woman he'd just met. What difference did it make how small town she thought he was?

"I love it," he answered, a hint of defensiveness under-cutting his words. "Ever since I was a kid, it's all I've ever wanted to be."

"Really?"

Nick's lips twisted. "You sound surprised." Like she couldn't understand how he wouldn't want something more.

"Not surprised. I guess, I'd say…envious."

"Envious?"

Darcy shrugged. "That you've always known without a doubt what you wanted to do."

He'd always known what *he* wanted, but that didn't mean he hadn't questioned what was best for his family. After Carol left, he'd gone to see her in San Francisco, willing to give up everything—his house, his practice, his home-town—to keep their family together. Only to discover his everything still wasn't enough for her.

"Yeah, I'm just lucky that way."

He wasn't sure what he'd given away with that comment, but Darcy's expression softened and she searched his face as if looking for some way inside him. That was not a place he wanted her, so he quickly asked, "What about you?"

He racked his memory for what he'd heard about her reasons for moving to Clearville. He was pretty sure he'd heard his sister, Sophia, talking about the woman renting the space two doors down from The Hope Chest. "You're opening a shop in town, right?"

As she went on to explain her boutique, a place where she would offer women advice on makeup, skin care and beauty treatments as well as sell the products along with candles and soaps in every scent imaginable, some of his skepticism must have shown on his face. "Why do I get the feeling," she asked, "that you're not going to be my first customer?"

Nick shrugged. "Sorry. It's just— Well, I've seen this all before."

Darcy set her mug on the counter with a dull thud. "Someone else has a shop like mine?"

"Not a shop just like it, but that spot you rented? It's gone through more changes in the past few years than I can remember. A dress shop, a shoe store, a health food clinic. Nothing stays open for long."

"So, you're telling me that the shop I've rented has some kind of Clearville Curse attached to it?" Darcy wiggled her fingers in a spooky motion, her teasing smile enough to jerk a rough half laugh out of Nick. But then a rush of heat surged through him when he remembered those same fingers pressed into his shoulders, and he quickly sobered.

"Not a curse, and it's not just Clearville, either. I'm sure it happens in small towns all over the place. Big-city folks get tired of the traffic and noise and fast pace of the city, so they go off seeking peace and quiet in some small town. Only before they've had the chance to even unpack, they start to miss all those same things they left behind. Before you know, they're gone without a word."

* * *

Darcy wasn't unaware of the chance she'd taken, and a string of failed stores could give a location a bad rap. Plus, starting a new business was always a risk, especially in this economy. But for as long as she could recall, her mother had talked about moving back to her hometown, only to never have the chance.

Darcy refused to miss her opportunity by waiting for the perfect moment. Instead she was going to make the most of the time she had now. Not that she was counting on blind faith to see her through. She'd done her research. Clearville was a small town, but one with a healthy tourist trade, catering to travelers who came to enjoy the surrounding redwoods, the rugged coastline, the days-gone-by feel of the Victorian Main Street.

The town had its share of bed-and-breakfasts, and Darcy had already arranged for a few of those businesses to carry her beauty baskets in their gift shops. She hoped to start up a buzz about The Beauty Mark before her grand opening.

"Maybe those other shops closed for a reason," she suggested.

"Such as?"

"So that the space would be available for me."

Nick stared at her as if he couldn't quite believe she was for real, and Darcy doubted she'd be able to explain her certainty in the move she'd made. Because even though she'd struggled with turn-of-the-last-century plumbing, ghostly electricity and a car that had turned into a lemon at the stroke of midnight, she refused to allow any of it to shake her faith that she was right where she was supposed to be.

Darcy's only regret was that her mother wasn't there with her, but she felt her presence in every decision she made. From their long-ago conversations as they'd imagined the perfect look and feel of the shop to the recent, far-more-practical hand Alanna had given her only child—the life insurance policy that made the dream a reality.

"I would think," she told Nick, "if anyone would understand, you might."

Nick's dark brows arched toward his hairline. Clearly he thought he'd be the *last* person to understand anything about her. "Me?"

"Yes, you said being a vet, being Clearville's vet, is the only thing you've ever wanted to be. It was the same thing for me the first time I drove down Main Street. I knew this was where I was supposed to be. It might have taken me a little longer to get here, but it's really the same. We're really the same."

Crossing his arms over his broad chest, Nick wryly countered, "We're really not. I was born here. I grew up here. This is all I've ever known."

"And I didn't just stumble across Clearville by accident. I may not be from here, but my family was," she said, feeling a little gratified by the surprise on his face. "My mother lived here until she and my grandparents moved when she was a teenager. She always dreamed about coming back and opening this boutique."

"Your mother always dreamed about it?"

"She did." Darcy didn't see the knowing look in his eyes until it was too late. "I mean, *we* did. It was *our* dream. It just turns out that I'm the one who's going to make it come true."

Seeing the unasked question in his gaze, she explained, "She was in a car accident a little over a year ago. Her injuries left her paralyzed. She was making progress, and I really thought if anyone had the strength to recover, she did. But then she suffered from a blood clot, and the doctor said there was nothing they could do."

"I'm sorry, Darcy."

Already figuring out Nick was a man of few words, she wasn't surprised when his condolences ended there. But she was touched when he took the mug she barely realized she was still holding and poured her a second cup of tea from the pot warming on the stove.

She soaked in the comfort of the small, thoughtful gesture and the heat from the steaming mug he handed back to her, but she wanted more. Nick stood close enough for the rain and earth clinging to his clothes to blend with the floral fragrance of the tea. But beneath that was the faint scent of his aftershave and warm male, and she longed to step closer and breathe it in…. To breathe him in….

He stepped back suddenly, leaving her holding nothing but the cup of tea.

It was only her vulnerability after talking about her mother that made his withdrawal feel like a rejection. It wasn't like he knew what she'd been thinking.

Please don't let him know what I was thinking….

"So your mother wanted to move back," Nick was saying as Darcy refocused on the words instead of simply following the movement of his lips.

She sighed, unsure why he was so hung up on that point. "This isn't only about my mother's last wish. It's about a new start for me. A chance for me to own the kind of store where I like to shop." She supposed she shouldn't be surprised by Nick's lack of interest. He wasn't exactly the demographic she had in mind for her boutique. "You know your sister's looking forward to my grand opening. I think Sophia's almost as excited as I am. And your daughter will love it. Girls always have a blast playing dress-up and having little girl makeovers—"

Warming to her subject, it took Darcy a minute to realize however slightly Nick had relaxed in the last few seconds, that moment was now gone. His expression was closed off, his posture once again rigid. He cut her off saying, "I should go check on the dog."

"I thought you said she was fine."

"She is."

Staring at the straight, unbending line of Nick's backbone as he walked away, Darcy couldn't help wondering, if the dog was okay, then what on earth was wrong with Nick Pirelli?

Chapter Three

Darcy bringing up his daughter and the dog's quick delivery of four tiny puppies could not have happened at a better time, Nick determined later as he watched the new pups, their eyes and ears still closed, their mouths wide open. The mama dog nuzzled them each in turn, guiding them toward their first meal.

"You're doing great, girl," he reassured her, and Nick could have sworn the dog responded with a proud smile.

He didn't know if Darcy truly was squeamish, but she had stayed away from the laundry room during the birthing process, giving Nick time to clean up and toss some of the old rags into the trash out back. She hadn't been in the kitchen as he'd passed through, and he hadn't gone looking for her.

"It's a big responsibility, you know," he murmured to the dog who'd either grown accustomed to his touch or had better things to worry about than the human petting her head. "Having a child is the most amazing experience and the most terrifying."

But he was determined to do right by Maddie. Which did not mean little girl makeovers. He didn't want Maddie growing up any faster than she already was, and no way was *he* ready for blush and mascara and highlights and God knows what else Darcy had in mind.

He'd been fighting with Carol for years about Maddie not being old enough to have her ears pierced. Even his mother and sister had taken his ex's side on that one.

"I was five when I had my ears pierced," Sophia had argued.

And she'd been eighteen when she left home.

Nick cringed at his line of thinking. Okay, not even he could make a direct correlation between ear piercing and taking off for parts unknown without admitting he sounded nuts, but still, the idea reinforced his plan to find a solid, wholesome influence for Maddie's life. Someone who could see his side of things and understand that his daughter belonged with him in Clearville.

Darcy was not that woman. Her decision to move to her mother's hometown, to make her mother's dream come true was admirable and touching...and misguided. But she'd have to learn that the hard way. Just as he had when he finally admitted getting married and raising a family in Clearville might have been his dream, but it hadn't been Carol's. Her dreams were bigger than small-town living, and Nick was sure Darcy's were, as well. Once reality set in, she'd figure that out.

Nick caught the scent of something fruity drifting over his shoulder. Was it one of her moisturizers or mud-mask thingies that made Darcy smell like a tropical, sun-kissed beach? If Darcy knew what she was talking about, women loved that kind of stuff. Somehow, though, he didn't think the explanation was that simple. He'd never had the desire to seek out the scent on any other woman's skin, to see if she tasted as good as she smelled....

He knew better than to turn around, feeling her presence there even before he heard her soft gasp.

"Oh, my— They're so tiny. Are they—?"

"They're fine. Perfectly healthy and good sized. Two boys and two girls." The boys took after mom with her blue merle coloring, but the girls must take after dear old dad with their smooth black coats. It was too soon to tell what the mix was, but Nick thought lab might be a good guess.

"Four," she breathed, and even though it wasn't possible, Nick swore he could feel her sigh drift like a caress over the exposed skin at the back of his neck. Chills raced down his spine, but he blamed the recent trip he'd made out into the storm. He'd ducked the rain as best he could, but clearly the collar of his shirt had gotten damp. It was the only reason why goose bumps were rising along every inch of skin.

"Better than eight," he answered, his tone more wry than he'd have liked.

"I can't even imagine. So what do you think?"

He tried keeping his gaze on the small family on the blanket in front of him, but he couldn't resist turning in Darcy's direction. He saw immediately the reason why she'd left the kitchen earlier. She'd changed out of the green shirt and jeans she'd worn into a pink softer-than-soft-looking jogging suit with a zippered jacket and drawstring bottoms. The potential ease of removal for both items was enough to run his mouth dry. To make matters worse, instead of being confined in a ponytail that kept the long strands away from her face, her hair now tumbled in voluptuous waves over her shoulders.

"What do I think about what?"

"What do you think we should name them?"

"I think that's up to you."

"But you delivered them. You were here when she needed you."

Her voice was soft as she gazed at him, and he had a hard time remembering she was talking about the dog. The warmth and gratitude in her gaze made Nick feel like puffing up his chest with pride. He didn't think he'd moved from his crouched position, but he would have sworn she was suddenly closer. Close enough for him to see her eyelashes were surprisingly, and naturally, darker than her hair. Close enough to see the faintest spray of freckles across her nose. Close enough for him to watch every movement of her tongue sliding across her pale pink lips.

The low rumble of thunder sounded from outside, and Nick jerked his attention away from Darcy's mouth and back to the request she'd made. "Stormy," he blurted out. "For one of the girls."

"Oh, how fitting. You said the girls were the little black ones?" At Nick's nod, Darcy said, "Then how about Cloud for the one of the gray boys?"

He suggested Rain for the other girl. "Which leaves one boy left."

Darcy's smile was full of mischievous laughter simply waiting to be unleashed, and Nick paused with an almost helpless feeling of anticipation to hear whatever she'd come up with.

"Bo," she announced suddenly.

He shook his head as if the word hadn't quite penetrated his brain. "Stormy, Rain, Cloud and...Bo?"

This time he had no doubt Darcy had leaned closer as she lowered her voice to share a secret. "It's short for Rainbow, but don't tell the other kids. They might make fun of him."

Rainbow. It was as silly and ridiculous as Nick had feared, still he couldn't help but give into laughter. Darcy's joined his, the masculine and feminine sound combining until, at once, all other sounds faded away. So, too, did the lighthearted energy in the tiny room, replaced by a growing awareness of how close they were, how isolated, with only the dogs inside and the lingering storm out.

"I should go." The statement, if not the words, were firm and decisive and utterly meaningless as Nick still didn't move.

Darcy swallowed. "You don't have to. It's still raining outside. I could fix some coffee."

But it wasn't coffee he was craving. Her scent called to him again, and this time Nick thought he recognized the summery mix of coconut and pineapple. He wondered if her skin would taste like piña colada if he kissed her.

He heard the faint catch in her breathing and the quicker rhythm that followed. He was less than a sigh away from claiming her lips with his own when the overhead bulb flickered. The light wasn't out for more than a split second, but when it came back on, the glare was like a flash of clarity illuminating the huge mistake he was about to make.

He didn't know if it was the storm, faulty wiring or fate stepping in to save him, but he jerked abruptly to his feet. The unexpected movement almost knocked Darcy back on her heels. He bent halfway—the gentleman his mother had taught him to be insisting he give her a hand, battling the survivor Carol had forced him to be warning him to stay far, far away. In the end he did nothing as Darcy pushed herself to her feet.

"I have to— This can't—" His mind formed the words, but his tongue tripped over them in his haste to say the exact opposite of what his body was feeling. "Look, I'm not interested in a fling or an affair or—"

Darcy's eyes widened, at first in shock, then in a growing realization and finally anger. "I offered you a cup of coffee, Dr. Pirelli, not a roll in the hay. You might be right and I don't know much about small towns, but where I come from coffee means coffee. If I was offering you sex, I would have said sex." The chill in her voice and fire in her eyes told him sex was nowhere near in the offering. "You can let yourself out when you're done here."

She brushed by him on her way through the kitchen and moments later, he heard a door slam somewhere from the back of the house. Nick exhaled a humiliated sigh of regret. Yes, he was definitely done here.

Nick stood in the middle of Darcy's kitchen feeling like he'd dodged a bullet, but guilty for winding up unscathed all the same. He was positive—almost positive—he hadn't imagined the heat and invitation in Darcy's gaze. She'd wanted him to kiss her, hadn't she? Hell, he'd been out of the game so long, he wasn't sure he still could read the signs. And damned if he didn't know if maybe all he saw was his *own* desire reflected in her eyes. But no matter what he saw or thought he saw, that didn't give him the right to hurt her with his clumsy rejection.

Yet what else could he have said? That she was a beautiful, sexy woman and he'd sleep with her in a heartbeat if he wasn't already looking for an entirely different kind of woman for his wife? A different kind of mother for Maddie? Somehow he didn't think that would have scored any points in her book either.

He thought briefly about apologizing, in a note left behind for her to find—because no way was he searching her out in her bedroom where he assumed she'd taken refuge—only to decide against it.

It was probably better to leave things as they were. If

he'd ticked her off as much as he thought he had, then he wouldn't have to worry about ending up on her radar again—except maybe for her to shoot some dirty looks in his direction on any rare occasion when their paths might cross.

He checked on the mama dog and her puppies one more time before he packed up his bag and left out the back door, the same way he'd come in. The slash of wind and rain pelting him the moment he stepped outside the warmth and comfort of Darcy's house felt like punishment, but the sudden chill was just what he needed. He didn't bother trying to outrun the storm on his way to his truck or duck for cover beneath the arms of the large tree in her front yard. Putting his head down, he methodically trudged along the gravel driveway.

A summer storm might not be what the term "cold shower" usually meant, but it would do.

The baseball game was likely over, but he couldn't have used a beer more. After fishing his keys from his front pocket, Nick turned the ignition and—nothing. Not a click. Not a flicker of light from the dash. Nothing.

Rain pounded on the roof of his SUV in a constant, unrelenting pattern as he reached for his phone. Cell coverage was always spotty at best thanks to the surrounding mountains. Add in the storm, and Nick shouldn't have been surprised when he got no reception. Dropping his wet head back on the padded headrest, he seriously debated sitting out the storm and the night in his truck. But what if Maddie needed him? His cell phone was as useless as his dead battery, and he needed to be at home in case she called.

It didn't happen so often anymore, but there'd been a time when Maddie brought back more than souvenirs and gifts from her trips to see her mother. Her first few nights back home, she used to wake up crying, her nightmares filled with terrors of being lost in the big city, trapped in falling elevators or stuck on escalators that carried her far, far away.

As much as he'd hated to see his daughter frightened, a small—very small—part of him had taken comfort in her needing her dad and the security and familiarity of small-town Clearville.

He didn't want to be out of contact from Maddie, not even for one night. Not even if it meant facing Darcy Dawson. He was soaked to the skin by the time he reached the front porch and knocked on the door.

"My battery's dead," he announced before she had the chance to launch into him for his nerve at showing his face on her doorstep. "I've got cables if I could just use your car for a—" He nearly swallowed his tongue to keep from using the word *jump*.

"Sorry," she said, arms crossed over her chest, "but you can't."

Nick snapped his jaw shut. Okay, so he'd known she might slam the door in his face. Half expected it, but he also thought once she heard what he needed, she'd oblige—just to get him and his vehicle off her property if for no other reason. "Look, I was a jerk."

"You were."

"A total jerk."

"Right."

His frustration mounting when Darcy refused to bend an inch, he snapped, "I'm trying to apologize here."

"Really?" Her elegant eyebrows shot upward. "Because—again where I come from—apologies usually start with the words 'I'm sorry' and end with 'Can you ever forgive me?'"

Clenching his jaw, Nick ground out the words from between gritted teeth. "I'm sorry, Darcy. Can you ever forgive me?"

He sounded about as sorry as when he was a kid and his father insisted any confrontations with his brothers ended in a handshake, but it was the best he could do. And he really didn't expect it to work.

Still Darcy did lower her arms and her posture loosened ever-so-slightly. "I'll think about it."

"So does that mean I can use your car?"

"No." She held up a hand before his head actually exploded. "Because my car isn't here. My car hasn't been here for days, ever since I left it at the mechanic's in town. So good luck getting a new battery."

Nick swore beneath his breath, but put the problem with his battery on the back burner for a second to address what Darcy had said about the garage in town. First, there was only one car shop in town. And second, it was owned by his youngest brother. Nick might have gotten on Sam's case over the years about his desire to live his life like Peter Pan, but his Lost Boy brother was a pure genius when it came to anything mechanical.

"Your car's been in the shop for days? Was there a part that needed to be ordered?" He couldn't imagine a problem Sam wouldn't be able to fix blindfolded with one hand tied behind his back.

"The mechanic told me what was wrong and what it would cost to fix it but—" Darcy shrugged as if that was the last she'd heard.

None of which sounded like Sam. His brother always followed through with a client if a job was going to take longer than anticipated. Most of the time, he beat any time frame he gave, especially since he'd recently hired on some help.

"But I shouldn't really complain. The mechanic has been

sweet enough to pick me up when I've needed to go into town."

"He's been giving you rides?"

That sounded more like Sam. With his teasing smile and lighthearted charm, his youngest brother had always had a way with women. *All* women. He never seemed to single out one in particular, and for him to put his reputation as a mechanic on the line for the pleasure of driving Miss Darcy—

Jealousy sizzled through Nick, eating away at logic and reason like acid.

"You're welcome to come in and use my phone. And by 'use my phone,' I mean *use my phone*. That's not any kind of big-city sexual innuendo."

The slap of humiliation heated his cheeks, but the only thing worse was knowing he deserved every moment Darcy spent raking him over the coals. "I'd appreciate it."

The words were too stiff, too formal, but he didn't know how else to pry his foot from his mouth other than to watch his every word. The same way he had back when his Nana Pirelli was still alive and he wasn't too big or too old for her to slap upside the head. But despite Darcy's insistence that her offer had nothing to do with sex, his mind went there anyway as he followed the seductive sway of her hips as she led the way into the house.

It was his first glimpse at the front of the house. Like the laundry area, the living room showed signs that Darcy had yet to unpack. The built-in bookcases flanking either side of the brick-faced fireplace were conspicuously empty. So, too, was the wall above the hearth, a large expanse crying out for a family portrait. Instead, six splotches of paint marred the space as if she was having a hard time deciding on a single color.

He had the feeling the furniture, mismatched floral

couches huddled around an old-fashioned steamer trunk, had come with the house. He wondered why Darcy would even bother redecorating. The paint would likely have yet to dry by the time she grew tired of small-town living and headed back to the city.

She handed him a cordless phone and disappeared through the doorway into the kitchen. Nick wasn't sure if she was trying to give him privacy or she'd simply rather not be in the same room with him. Sighing, he dialed his brother's number. His brother Drew's number. Sam would have been the logical choice, but logic wasn't running real high at the moment. His call went through to voice mail, though, giving Nick little choice but to call Sam who also asked him to leave a message and told him he'd call back later.

Swearing beneath his breath, Nick disconnected the call. After his brothers, his soon to be brother-in-law would be Nick's next choice, but Jake had taken Sophia to L.A. to introduce her to his mother and stepfather. His parents would have gone to bed hours ago, and he'd hate to get them out of bed at this time of night.

"You could always call a cab."

The helpful suggestion came from the kitchen, letting Nick know Darcy had picked up on his frustration even though he hadn't said a word. "Clearville doesn't have a cab company."

"That was a joke, Doc." Framed by the doorway, Darcy crossed her arms over her chest. Backlit by the light from the kitchen, her red hair shimmered with an ethereal, almost halo effect. But the gleam in her green eyes was anything but angelic as she added, "You probably won't find this funny, either, but you're welcome to spend the night."

Spend the night with Darcy Dawson.

Proving he was at least smart enough not to make the

same mistake twice, Nick didn't assume she was offering him anything more than a place to crash. But even the thought of sleeping under the same roof, with Darcy only a room away, seemed far too dangerous. It had been a long time, way too long, since Nick had spent the night with a beautiful, desirable woman. If he had any other choice—

Looking down at the phone still in his hand, he said, "My daughter's spending the night at a friend's. I need to let her know how to reach me."

At his words, Darcy seemed to unbend a little, far more so than she'd done at his admittedly lame apology. "Of course," she said as she backed out of the doorway, leaving him to make the call in private.

Dialing the Martins' number from memory, he immediately apologized when MaryAnne answered. "Hey, Mary-Anne, it's Nick."

"Oh, Nick. Hi." The woman sounded slightly surprised.

"Sorry to call so late. I just wanted to let you know that my cell phone's reception is down. I don't like being out of touch in case Maddie needs me, so I wanted to give you a landline number. I'm…taking care of an emergency call."

"Oh, an *emergency*. Right. Of course."

It had to be his guilty conscience that made it seem like MaryAnne had stressed the word, almost as if she suspected he was lying. "Yeah. Anyway, I'll, um, be at this number for the rest of the night." He recited the number Darcy had given him and apologized again, saying, "I hope I didn't wake you."

MaryAnne laughed, sounding more like herself. "Don't you know by now that the whole point of a sleepover is *not* sleeping?"

Nick winced at the very idea of being surrounded by half-a-dozen preteen girls, amped up on sugar and a lack of sleep. "I owe you, big-time."

"Just remember that when Fluffy's shots come due."

"You got it," Nick promised. "Fluffy is on the house."

He ended the call while a movement from the corner of his eye caught his attention as Darcy stepped into the room, her arms full of sheets and pillows. Her brows rose in question as she padded barefoot across the scuffed hardwood floors and dumped everything on the couch. "Fluffy is on the house?"

"The Martins' cat," he explained. The cross-eyed Siamese may well have been fluffy, but Nick had long thought the feline's name should have been something even more appropriate like "Butch" or "Killer" or "Devil's Spawn." Still, he'd rather take on a dozen hissing, scratching fluffballs than host a sleepover for his daughter and five of her friends.

"Is there a lot of bartering done for work around here?"

"Sometimes," he answered, feeling defensive even though Darcy's question had been more curious than amused. It was part of small-town living. Times were hard, and people helped out where they could. That sense of community, of neighbors lending a hand, made Clearville... well, Clearville. Despite the occasional downside of everyone knowing everyone else's business, Nick had always appreciated how the town's citizens looked out for their own.

He waited, half expecting, half dreading another sexual innuendo comment. He could see one written in the sparkle of her green eyes, but maybe she'd decided to cut him some slack after all because she simply made up the couch. His gaze locked on every movement—how she bent at the waist and the pale pink material stretched across her perfect backside, how she reached to tuck the sheet behind the couch cushions and the strip of creamy skin peeked out above the hem of her sweatpants, how her hands smoothed over the soft cotton sheets...

If he hadn't been tongue-tied before, he certainly was now. The last thing he needed was to try to fend off another one of her teasing remarks. It didn't matter that she wasn't serious or that he deserved her giving him a hard time. Because even the harmless banter punched holes in the shoddy patchwork job he'd done when Carol had left, revealing the empty, aching hollow he'd been trying to hide—for Maddie's sake, for his family's, but mostly for his own almost desperate self-preservation. If no one knew how much Carol's desertion had ripped away from him, then he didn't have to admit it—not even to himself.

He didn't have what it took to laugh with a woman like Darcy anymore—if he ever had. That he shouldn't *want* to flirt with her made no difference. Knowing he couldn't, knowing he'd fail miserably, was what mattered. He'd end up seeing the same pity in her gaze as he'd seen in Carol's when he had showed up in San Francisco with his offer to move there to keep their family together. The very thought threatened to fill the emptiness inside him with a sickening mix of humiliation and failure until the unfeeling void seemed like a blessing.

So he was glad, really, that Darcy was giving him a break.

But when she gave the floral pillow a final pat and turned to face him, Nick thought maybe he'd breathed a sigh of relief a little too soon.

"So how do you decide fair compensation," she asked, "for say—the local vet delivering four puppies?"

Refusing to respond to her teasing, he quoted his normal rate for a house call even though it made him feel like an ass. The straight man who couldn't bend enough to enjoy a joke.

Darcy sighed and shook her head in disappointment, but that was still better than the pity he might have seen. "I was really hoping you might go for some soothing candles or a relaxation massage."

Yeah, right. Like the very idea of Darcy's hands on him would be relaxing in the least. He could already feel the tension stretching to all points inside him, warning him that, at some time, his tightly leashed control was going to break. He could only hope he'd be far, far away from Darcy Dawson when it happened.

"I'll be sure to write you a check then," she said, a little of her teasing fading away, and damned if he didn't miss that spark in her eyes already. "I laid out a few things in the bath down the hall for you to get cleaned up," she added with a nod at his still damp and slightly muddy clothes. "Sleep tight, Doc."

He thought he might have mumbled a good-night but was too busy escaping into the bathroom to stick around for a more formal response. He felt like she'd given him an out, and he was taking it. Shutting the door, he leaned back against the panel.

Like the rest of the house, the bath showed its age with pale blue throughout—tub, tile, toilet and sink. He might not know Darcy well, but she was clearly a woman of style. A woman like Carol. His ex-wife had insisted he gut the entire interior of the first house they bought in Clearville, enlisting his brother Drew's help behind Nick's back when she thought he wasn't working fast enough. And yes, Drew was a contractor and amazing at his job, but dammit, it was supposed to be *their* house—Carol's and Nick's. Not Carol's and Nick's and Drew's, no matter how much he loved his brother.

Shaking off the memories, Nick reached for the towel she'd left on the edge of the tub and a bundle of clothes fell to the blue and white mosaic floor. As he bent to pick them up, he found a T-shirt and sweats, but nothing like the pink feminine pair Darcy wore. The worn T-shirt was an extra large with the Trail Blazers emblem faded across the front, the pants slate gray and masculine.

Nick's hands fisted in the soft material. He could tell himself all he wanted that he didn't care who or how many men Darcy had dated, but when he was faced with the proof, the truth hit like a blow to the gut. He cared too damn much.

The last thing he wanted was to put on clothes left behind by some other guy. His own muddy clothes and, hell, even the bucket seat of his truck were looking better and better. With a muttered curse, he attacked the buttons on his shirt. He was making way too big of a deal out of something that could only amount to nothing.

He changed as quickly as he could, as if—like taking medicine—the faster it went down, the easier it was to swallow. He hit the lights and made his way back to the living room. He breathed a sigh of relief that Darcy was nowhere to be seen, but her voice still rang in his ears as he crossed the room.

Sleep tight, Doc.

Pulling back the sheets tucked into the couch pillows, he lay down as if stretching out on a bed of nails. He closed his eyes tight as if *that* could somehow erase the sight, the sound, the—

His eyes popped open as the faint promise of something citrusy and sweet drifted over him. Nick still didn't know what it was that made Darcy smell like a summer's day after a hard, cold winter, but enough of the scent clung to the softness of the sheets for him to feel like she was lying there beside him.

His jaw clenched. It was going to be a long, long night.

Chapter Four

A normal woman, put in the position of having a strange man sleeping under her roof, might have been worried. Since Darcy was very much a "normal" woman, then the blame—or really, the credit—had to go to Nick. Who, although she didn't know him well, wasn't a strange man.

He was one of the good guys.

She'd expected as much after getting to know his sister, Sophia, who managed an antiques shop only a few doors down from the spot Darcy had rented. Sophia had recently moved back to her hometown with her fiancé, and the dark-haired, dark-eyed woman practically glowed with happiness. She'd admitted growing up in the small town hadn't always been easy, but Clearville was home, and nothing was more important to the Pirellis than family.

Even without Sophia's words, Darcy had her own proof of that last night.

She hadn't intended to eavesdrop on Nick's phone call,

but she'd walked in during the middle of the conversation. The concern and thoughtfulness of calling to check on his daughter and to make sure the little girl could get in touch with him showed where his priorities lay. The thought of a soft-hearted father hidden behind the strong, unbending facade was almost enough to make Darcy's own heart melt a little, though she tried hard not to let it show.

Not when she already knew how Nick, and most likely the rest of the good guys in town, undoubtedly saw her.

I'm not interested in a fling or an affair.

As if that was all she was interested in.

The truth was, Darcy had very much wanted to settle down, to get married and start a family. She thought she was well on her way when she had met Aaron. Only, as it turned out, he wanted to succeed in politics even more. When he feared she'd be more of a liability than an asset, he'd quickly gone out and found a woman more suitable for the picture-perfect family in his future.

Though their breakup was for the best and she was lucky it had happened before the marriage and children she'd imagined, Darcy couldn't pretend Aaron's rejection hadn't hurt. Hadn't shaken her confidence.

But it had also lifted the weight of expectation off her shoulders, and she'd felt free. Riding high on her decision to move to Clearville and pursue her mother's dream, she'd been more than a little giddy. Like a kid who'd cast off training wheels, she'd let a little bit of that freedom go to her head and had taken her first few curves a little too fast. No surprise, really, that she'd already crashed.

It had all seemed so harmless when the handyman she'd hired had flirted outrageously with her. Flattered by the attention, Darcy had made the mistake of agreeing to go out with Travis Parker.

Throwing off the covers, she wished she could toss

Travis's memory aside as easily. The outdoor guide/part-time handyman was handsome, but his arrogance quickly stripped away any attraction Darcy might have felt. His cocky belief that saying yes to a third date with him was the same as saying yes to sex put an immediate end to their final evening together. Or so she'd thought.

Only later did she realize she'd done more than bruise Travis's knuckles when she slammed the front door shut on his hand. Not about to admit he hadn't gotten over the threshold, let alone beyond first base, Travis had spread the story about Darcy being an easy city girl. At least, she was pretty sure that was where the rumor started. How much each of her subsequent dates added on to enhance their own reputations, she didn't know.

She told herself she didn't care and might have even believed it—until Nick.

Because, truthfully, he was right. She had been offering more than coffee. She'd been offering him the chance to stay, asking him to share a little longer the quiet intimacy they'd found sitting side by side on her laundry room floor, inviting him to relax, to laugh…

And when he'd practically jumped out of his skin to get away from her— Yeah, that had hurt.

But when he'd been forced to come back to her doorstep and ask for *her* help… Well, tossing his words back in his face had been the most fun she'd had with the opposite sex in quite some time. His embarrassment had gone a long way toward dousing her anger. And even though he hadn't lightened up enough to respond, now and then she'd caught a hint of something inside him—an answering spark that told her he'd wanted to snap back, to have some fun, to flirt.…

But then the walls had come back up, as if he'd cut off the possibility.

Because of her and the reputation she had? Or was it because of something in Nick's past? Probably a combination of the two, but if she had to guess, she'd say those walls weren't anything new. They were beaten and battle scarred from holding the world at bay for a long, long time, and she wondered when the last time was that Nick Pirelli had let anyone in.

Taking a deep breath, she met her own gaze in the bathroom mirror. She'd taken far more pains than she normally would have on a Saturday morning in selecting a turquoise tunic belted over black leggings. It was a casual outfit, but a little dressier than needed when her plans for the day included unpacking more of the boxes arriving at her house on a daily basis and organizing what would soon be the inventory for her store. Not that Nick would be all that impressed with the way her silver-link belt matched her bracelet or with the way the blue-green color of her shirt brought out the emerald in her eyes.

Even if she hadn't misread the desire in his eyes last night as they crouched together next to the mama dog and her puppies, he had made his feelings more than clear. Trendy clothes weren't going to change his mind. She wasn't sure anything would, but she was determined to hold her head high and put her best foot—and fashionable sandal—forward, no matter what Nick thought of her.

Decision made, Darcy snapped off the bathroom light. She headed down the hall toward the living room where she saw the sheets and clothes she had laid out for him the night before neatly folded on the arm of the couch. She hadn't even realized she had brought along some of Aaron's clothes until she'd started unpacking. Her plan was to donate the few items, but she hadn't gotten around to it yet.

Darcy picked up the T-shirt, waiting for the feeling of hurt and anger to swamp her like it usually did when she saw the reminders of her past. But the shirt no longer held the hint of Aaron's cologne, but the simpler, more basic scent of soap and something far more complicated and less easily defined that smelled like…Nick.

The unwanted memories didn't come, almost as if Nick had somehow wiped away what no longer was with the possibility of what could be.

Shaking off the fanciful thought, she dropped the clothes back on the couch. Expecting to find Nick checking on the dog, she walked into the kitchen, but it, too, was empty.

Almost empty, she amended as her gaze landed on the mother dog happily nursing her babies in the small laundry area off the kitchen.

Despite the overwhelming thought of five dogs in her house—*five dogs*—Darcy couldn't help smiling. There was something so maternal about the act and something so undeniably sweet and helpless about the pups that she wondered if she may yet overcome her fears. Stepping closer, she toed the edge of the doorway.

The water and food bowls were freshly filled. "I see someone checked on you before taking off at least."

Her own voice sounded loud in the empty kitchen, almost as if she were talking to herself and yet…not. With the dog's upright ears and fascinating two-colored eyes, she could believe the animal understood every word she said.

The dog cocked its head, almost as if sizing up the competition for the handsome vet's attention, and Darcy wryly added, "I don't think you have anything to worry about, girl. He clearly likes you better than he likes me."

Overcast skies lingered from the storm the night before, giving the whole world a grayish hue. Rain still dripped from the trees overhead and Darcy's gravel drive had turned into a giant puddle. By late afternoon, the haze would likely burn off and the ground would start to dry, but Nick planned to be long gone by then.

After suffering through the night, jerking in and out of dreams where he walked down the hall to Darcy's bedroom and joined her on an endless bed of cloud-soft satin, he had little compunction about sneaking out at the break of dawn. He was tired, hungover from lack of sleep, and he knew damn well his resistance was at an all-time low. He was afraid if she made one teasing, sexy comment, she'd see in his hungry gaze every half-awake, half-asleep fantasy he'd had the night before.

In even this faintest light of day, he was now certain he'd imagined the come-on in her gaze last night, that her offer of coffee had been nothing more than an offer of coffee, and he'd made a total ass out of himself with his nearly virginal protest.

God, he was an idiot! If the two-mile hike into town was what it would take to get his butt home, then he deserved every soggy step along the way. But as he leaned against his good-for-nothing SUV, the rumble of a diesel engine broke through the faint drip of lingering rainwater and birdsong. Nick watched Sam's tow truck chug down the small street. What had Darcy told him last night? How *sweet* the mechanic had been, giving her rides into town when she needed them?

Yeah, well, Nick would see just how sweet Sam was this morning about making sure *he* had a ride to town and that Darcy's car would be fixed and back in her driveway today.

The tension drained from his shoulders and his hands unclenched as he caught sight of the mechanic behind the wheel. It was not his brother, but instead the teenager Sam had hired to work with him over the summer. The tow truck pulled up behind Nick's SUV, but Willson Gentry didn't immediately climb out. While Sam taking on an employee had caught Nick by surprise, his brother's choice of apprentice had not. The seventeen-year-old kid had been hanging out at Sam's garage after school, eager to learn all he could about cars, long before he could even drive.

From what Sam said, the teenager had a quick mind, picking up everything Sam taught him—something a few folks in town might have found hard to believe, thanks to Will's extreme shyness. It was no surprise that the quiet, awkward boy had taken one look and fallen hard for Darcy Dawson or that Darcy would see the boy as sweet.

Hell, if Nick had followed Willson's M.O. and kept his own mouth shut, he'd have been better off. "Hey, Willson," Nick said as the boy finally climbed from the oversize cab.

Ducking his head and hiding beneath the brim of his baseball cap, Will mumbled something Nick took as a hello. "I came by to help out Ms. Dawson with her dog, and when I went to leave, my battery was dead," he said casually, cutting out a few details along the way—like that his attempt to leave had taken place the night before. "She said she's been having some car trouble, too."

Nick couldn't see much of Will's face, but his ears, left exposed by the baseball cap, turned bright red. Taking pity on the kid, Nick said, "I told her my brother's shop is the best around and I'm *sure* her car will be fixed and back in her driveway by the end of the day, right?"

The bill of Will's cap bobbed once. Pushing away from his SUV, Nick said, "Good. Now that that's settled, I need a jump start and to get back to town."

He had to give Will credit. The kid knew his stuff, and Nick's SUV was soon running without a problem. As he was climbing into the front seat, Will spoke for the first time.

"You, um, won't say nothing, will you?"

Nick read the worry on the kid's face through the still

open driver's side door, his blue eyes big in a fair-skinned face that still held a few freckles from childhood. Nick didn't know what Will was more concerned about—Nick saying something to Sam…or Nick saying something to Darcy. Either way, it didn't matter. He had no intention of talking or even thinking about the past twelve hours again. "Not a word. But Ms. Dawson's car—"

"In her driveway. Today."

"Nothing to talk about then, is there?"

Will nodded again, but as his lovesick gaze drifted over to the small house, he gave an audible sigh. Slamming shut the SUV door, Nick drove off with his own focus straight out the windshield in front of him.

"Thanks again for watching her overnight," Nick said to MaryAnne Martin as he stepped into her living room.

"Oh, you're welcome." The short brunette smiled, her eyes bright and sharp despite what had to have been a sleepless night, judging from the sound of a half-dozen preteen girls still giggling upstairs. MaryAnne eyed him closely. "Looks like you had quite a night, too. What was that emergency again?"

"A, um, dog owner with a mama dog having her first litter." He told himself MaryAnne's curiosity was only that—interest in a vet emergency that had kept him out overnight. His own conscience was adding sexual innuendo that didn't exist. "But everything turned out okay. Two boys and two girls."

The clomp of footsteps down the hardwood stairs preempted MaryAnne's response as his daughter came down. A recent growth spurt had erased the last stages of babyhood, leaving behind an almost gangly girl who reminded him of a young colt—all long limbs and awkward joints seeming to work independent of each other. He winced at the clatter on the stairs, but fortunately it was only Maddie lugging a pale pink suitcase behind her, and not the sound of her tumbling down the stairs. The luggage had been Carol's idea, as if their daughter was a world traveler instead of a little girl whose belongings could have fit just as easily in her school backpack.

"Hey, honey." Nick tried not to wince as he caught sight of his daughter.

Her dark brown hair was sectioned off with multicolored ribbons woven into a dozen tiny braids. He'd learned far more about ponytails, pigtails and braids than he even thought he'd know as a thirty-three-year-old man, but he was already cringing at the thought of trying to untangle the knots she'd tied into her shoulder-length hair.

"Ready to go?"

She nodded, and before he could remind her to thank her hostess, Maddie dropped the handle of her suitcase and threw her skinny arms around the woman's plump waist. "Thanks, Mrs. Martin."

"You're welcome, sweetie." MaryAnne dropped a kiss onto his daughter's head, an act completely casual and comfortable.

His own mother was the same way, a hugger who expressed her love so easily. He could imagine his sister, Sophia, would be like that when her own child was born. Was it a female thing? Nick wondered. Something that came so naturally to women but seemed so forced whenever he tried to show his daughter any affection? He loved Maddie with his whole heart, but he'd never lost the awkwardness that plagued him from the moment she was born. When she first came home from the hospital, she'd been so tiny, so fragile. He'd had to be so careful of his every move, unable to ever fully relax or shake free of the fear of doing something wrong, of failing.

Maddie wasn't a newborn anymore, but as he watched her cling to MaryAnne, his failure to keep their family together made his stomach churn.

Hoping to cover his own discomfort, he reached for the hot-pink handle on his daughter's luggage. "I've got it, Dad," Maddie insisted, breaking away from MaryAnne's hug to grab the suitcase.

The show of independence, even the use of the term *Dad* instead of the more recent *Daddy,* had Nick holding back a sigh. Thanking MaryAnne again, he held open the door for his daughter, half expecting her to insist she was the type of woman to open her own door.

Once they were on their way in the SUV, he asked, "Did you have fun?"

Twirling the end of one braid, Maddie mumbled, "Uh-huh."

"What did you girls do? Other than each other's hair?"

She turned to him then, her brown eyes wounded. "You don't like it?"

"Sure, it's…colorful."

The lame compliment didn't get him very far, and Maddie slumped back in her seat. Trying again, he asked, "So, Mrs. Martin said you all stayed up pretty late…. You must have done something. Watched movies? Played games?"

"We just did stuff. You know."

No, and that was part of the problem. Nick couldn't get a handle on the kind of stuff that interested Maddie now. He wouldn't say it had ever been easy, but there'd been a time, not long ago, when cartoons, stuffed animals and dolls had fully captured his daughter's imagination. Now, though, she spent more time on the phone or playing video games or listening to music with her headphones on.

Shutting him out. Of course Nick remembered when Sophia was the same age that it was all a part of little girls growing up. But it didn't ease the fear of loss building inside him, the worry that one day he'd reach for Maddie and his daughter would slip through his fingertips.

"So what do you want to do today?" Though he was never completely off the clock, on call even when the office was closed, Nick tried to keep his weekends free for Maddie. "We could go see the movie in town."

"We saw it before I left to visit Mommy." She sighed as if he couldn't remember that far back.

What he remembered was when she used to want to see any kids' movie that came to the theater half a dozen times without ever tiring of it. But now...

"There are like a hundred movie theaters in San Francisco with all these huge screens and they have *all* the new movies, not just one."

Nick's hands tightened on the wheel. "I know, Maddie. Isn't it great that you get to go there and visit?"

He hoped his words didn't sound as if he'd had to chew them up like nails and spit them out, but that was certainly how it felt. No matter what his feelings for Carol, he refused to use his daughter as a pawn or try to make her choose sides. He only wished he could be sure his ex was following the same rules.

Hitting the edge of town, Maddie sighed again. "It's so *boring* here. There's nothing to do."

"That's not true. You just spent last night with your friends. Was that boring? And you're going to be helping your aunt Sophia with her wedding. You get to be the flower girl. I wouldn't call that *nothing.*"

Maddie gazed out the window, and he couldn't be sure anything he said made a difference in her eyes. He'd been through this all before. The churning in his gut turned into a full-bore tidal wave of worry and doubt. He recognized his own words all too well. Just as he recognized Maddie's.

Because, although the voice belonged to his daughter, the words were definitely Carol's. And if his argument hadn't worked with Carol, did he really think it would sway their daughter?

In the end, the offer to go for ice cream pacified Maddie for the moment. Proving he would never understand the female mind, not even an eight-year-old's, he stood outside the shop while his "Clearville is so boring" daughter ate her vanilla cone. Despite a decent variety offered by the shop, Maddie never went for Double Chocolate Chunk or Very Berry Swirl. Once in a while, she'd ask for some sprinkles, but no matter what, she always wanted vanilla.

He'd already downed a single scoop of chocolate mint, but he didn't mind waiting while Maddie slowly licked the creamy rivulets from the softening dessert. He'd learned the hard way that kids, car rides and ice cream cones didn't mix, having cleaned the sticky, melting substance off his dash more than once.

Taking a look around, he smiled at the typical Saturday afternoon in downtown Clearville. Store owners had moved some displays outside to entice shoppers into their stores and to take advantage of the warm weather. Tourists walked up and down the street, cameras in hand to take photos of the Victorian houses. He could see a steady stream of shoppers coming in and out of The Hope Chest, the antiques store his sister had managed for the owner, Hope Daniels. With Sophia and her fiancé, Jake Cameron, still out of town, Nick assumed Hope was running the place herself today.

He carefully averted his gaze from the empty shop a few doors down, but that didn't stop him from wondering if Will had returned Darcy's car. If she'd driven into town... If she was inside right now, planning her displays for mud masks and herbal moisturizers and whatever else she planned to sell.

We're really alike.

Nick snorted, glad he'd already finished his ice cream so he didn't have mint chip coming out his nose. Alike, yeah, right. Big-city girls and small-town boys had nothing in common. Carol had taught him that. His gaze slid to his own small-town girl, and he shook his head. Wild, multicolored braids and plain vanilla ice cream. He really didn't understand the female mind at all.

He'd just passed Maddie a napkin—she was far beyond the days when he used to wipe her sticky face and hands—when the sound of laughter reached his ears.

"Morning, Nick!"

Glancing over with a puzzled frown, he spotted three women he recognized as mothers of the girls at Maddie's slumber party. "Morning, ladies."

Another ripple of laughter followed, and the mint chip he'd eaten seemed to settle like a block of ice in his gut.

"We hear you had an *emergency* call last night, Doc!"

An emergency call. That was what he had told Mary-Anne Martin when he phoned her from Darcy's house.

The marvels of modern technology, Nick thought grimly. Even in tiny Clearville, the Martins cared enough about *their* privacy to have caller ID. Too bad MaryAnne didn't care nearly as much about his. Just how many people had she told about him spending the night at Darcy's?

He still remembered the whispers, the curious and open stares from his time with Carol. First when he married her out of the blue and then, four years later, when she'd taken off pretty much the same way. He'd hated it then, and he'd done everything he could since to stay out of the Clearville limelight and out of the tangled mess of the local grapevine.

Until now—

A faint tinkling chime echoed down the street, and Nick knew where the sound had come from. But knowing didn't stop him from looking anyway, and he watched as Darcy pushed open her shop door and stepped out.

The turquoise shirt she wore faithfully followed each curve from her breasts to just below her hips, where black leggings embraced the longest pair of legs he'd ever seen. Her hair was pulled back in a high ponytail, waving in the breeze like some kind of red flag, and every ounce of testosterone in his body was urging him to charge.

As if she could feel his gaze, she glanced over in his direction. Their eyes met, and even from across the street, the impact hit hard—a swift kick of desire straight to his gut that had him sucking in a quick breath.

Just the sight of her sent him back to that moment in her kitchen. A moment that he still couldn't decide had really happened or was only in his imagination. But he did know one thing for sure—he should have kissed her. Whether she'd been waiting for him to or not, he should have kissed her. If he had, he wouldn't be standing here, watching and wondering... He'd *know*.

But the laughter was there again, reminding Nick that he and Darcy weren't the only two people in the world. For a brief moment he'd forgotten about the giggling trio. He'd even forgotten about Maddie. A cold splash of guilt put his priorities back in order, and he glanced down at his daughter, who had been too busy chasing melting drips of ice cream down her cone to notice his lapse.

He'd noticed, though. Darcy had that effect on him— making him forget his goal, making him lose sight of what was most important. And so what if, for that split second of time, he'd felt like a man interested in a woman? A man caught in the rush of a new, exciting attraction? A man free from worry of the future and the scars of the past? So what?

He was not that man. He was a single father, worried and scarred. "You almost done, Maddie?"

"Uh-huh."

She hardly ever ate the whole cone, but that didn't mean he could ever talk her into getting a cup. "All right, then. Go throw that soggy mess away."

As his daughter went over to the trash can, he focused on a small billboard in front of the shop. Alongside advertisements of the flavor of the month, people had pinned various notices into the corkboard surface. A few help-wanted posts. An announcement about his sister's upcoming wedding. A found dog poster...

He stepped closer to the bulletin board. Beneath the words *Found Dog* was a photo of the blue merle cattle dog who'd had her litter of puppies in Darcy's laundry room.

Darcy had been telling the truth. The mama dog didn't belong to her. And she wasn't irresponsible. She was kind enough to take in a stray and try to find its owners, and he'd given her a hard time for it.

Just one more thing to apologize for, Nick thought.

He looked back in Darcy's direction a minute later when he heard the scrape of metal against concrete. Shaking his head, he watched as she awkwardly maneuvered a six-foot ladder out the doorway. She made too sharp a turn, hit the bottom of the ladder against the doorjamb, had to back up and try again. She cleared the doorway the second time around—barely.

Seriously, what did she think she was doing?

Not just wrestling with a ladder in front of a shop on Main Street, but what was she doing in Clearville? This might be where her family was from, but it certainly wasn't where she belonged. It was so obvious to Nick, he didn't understand how she couldn't see for herself that she didn't fit in.

This was Small Town, U.S.A. People around here liked things plain and simple and quiet.

You like things plain and simple and quiet, his conscience mocked, but deep down, Nick wasn't even sure that was true. Maybe he'd simply spent enough years telling himself that, he'd finally believed it. And it had taken meeting Darcy to tear off the blinders and for him to see what he really wanted.

And what he really couldn't have.

Chapter Five

It was a good thing, Darcy decided as she stretched as far as she could from the top of the ladder, that she was afraid of dogs and not heights or she would never get the banner hung above her shop.

The midmorning sun warmed her skin between hints of a cool breeze that teased the hair she'd swept into a high ponytail and made the pink vinyl banner dance in her hand. The right side had been easy. She'd maneuvered the ladder up against the side of the building and slipped the grommet in her "Grand Opening" sign over the hook. But the left side—

She shifted on the rung, the muscles in her arms and legs stretching as she tried to extend her reach a little more without losing her balance.

The left side of her shop had a built-in planter filled with a beautiful mix of pink and purple petunias, silvery dusty miller and top-heavy snapdragons, loaded with purple and yellow blooms. She loved the colorful display, but with the brick flower box in the way, she couldn't move the ladder as close as it needed to be. Which meant reaching out over the planter on her tiptoes, one hand clinging to the top rung, the other grasping the bright pink banner, and—

Yes, got it!

The last little "umph" of effort scraped metal against brick, and Darcy clung precariously to the ladder, her heart pounding with triumph and potential disaster as she regained her balance once again.

She'd just caught her breath when a pair of strong hands circled her waist, swinging her off the ladder and setting her back with both feet on the ground. She spun around, her protest dying when she saw Nick Pirelli. That feeling of flying through the air and heading for a fall came back full force at she met his gaze. "Nick! You nearly gave me a heart attack."

If possible the scowl on his face darkened further at her words, his brows lowering deeper over his eyes. "What the hell do you think you're doing? Have you lost your mind?"

Her face started to heat at his shouted criticism. Okay, so that final stretch when the tiptoes of her left foot were about the only thing touching the ladder wasn't the smartest move she'd made, but she wasn't crazy.

Unless…

"Is that part of the Clearville Curse?"

"The what?"

"The curse on my shop."

The reminder of the conversation they'd had in her kitchen sent a wash of red climbing up his neck. The bit of embarrassment served him right as far as Darcy was concerned. She deserved a little lighthearted revenge even if seeing Nick with his daughter in front of the ice cream shop had diffused any lingering hurt feelings.

Darcy had known he was a single father with custody of his little girl. But knowing and seeing were two different things. Seeing Nick with his daughter made what sounded like a brush-off the night before a more legitimate explanation, even if the delivery had been completely awkward and insulting. His determination to put his daughter first only made him that much more attractive—and unobtainable.

Nick glanced over her shoulder at the still empty shop. "I told you—"

"All about how the shop has gone through a suspicious number of renters," Darcy interrupted, keeping her expression serious despite the smile threatening to break free. "Is that what happens? They all go insane?"

Throwing up his hands in aggravation, he said, "There is no curse!"

Darcy exhaled on a big sigh. "Well, thank goodness for that. You had me worried with all your 'doom and gloom' talk."

Nick stared at her, looking as though he couldn't decide if he wanted to laugh at her...or kiss her. And suddenly Darcy knew. She hadn't imagined the attraction between them last night. Nick might not want to want her...but he still did.

Darcy swallowed as the awareness stretched between them, announcing that attraction as obviously as the banner snapping and dancing in the breeze above her shop. Nick finally broke the tension, glancing down the street. He muttered something about collecting his daughter at The Hope Chest, ready to pull another disappearing act, Darcy was sure. Only...she didn't want him to go.

Unobtainable, her conscience reminded her. She'd already made the mistake of diving too deep into a relationship with Aaron. She'd been in over her head long before she realized he was still standing safely on the shore. The next time she fell in love, she didn't want to be the only one risking her heart, and a guarded, cautious man like Nick wasn't the type to take chances.

He would keep a safe distance away while she would be the one to get too close and end up getting burned.

But that wasn't enough to stop her from backing toward the open doorway. "Let me give you the grand tour first. I'll only take a minute."

Darcy decided not to read too much into the little skip of happiness her heart took when Nick followed her inside. "Right now, it doesn't look like much," she admitted, knowing the shop looked exactly like what it was—a small space that had been empty far too long.

"But I was sold on the store's location and the built-ins," she said with a wave at the rows of waist-high shelving. The displays would be perfect for showcasing products while the cabinets below would store additional inventory. "Remove the carpet, add some fresh paint on the shelves and walls, install some beadboard wainscoting along the back wall, and you won't recognize this place."

Nick looked around the shop, but Darcy had the feeling he wasn't picturing the place filled with beauty products and customers the way she was. "Are you hiring Travis Parker to do the work?" he asked, his focus still on the surrounding four walls.

"Uh, no. I'm not interested in seeing Travis professionally or personally." Darcy wasn't sure what made her share that information, since Nick hadn't exactly asked, but at least now it was out there. Just in case he cared. "We went on a couple of meaningless dates, that was all."

Even if she wasn't still dodging the grabby handyman's calls, Darcy wouldn't have hired him. Tackling the century-old plumbing and electrical at her house had been too risky a job for her amateur skills. But the facelift on The Beauty

Mark—that she could handle. She and her mother had done their share of DIY work, a trial-and-error process that included consulting with orange-vested hardware store employees, dummy books and online sites.

Thanks to their success in the past, she'd seen beyond the run-down appearance of the space she'd rented. She'd looked at the threadbare carpeting and imagined the hardwood floors beneath, gleaming under new layers of stain. She'd pictured the pockmarked walls covered with beadboard wainscoting, topped by a row of chair rail and brightened by fresh paint.

"I'm not looking to hire anyone. My mom and I moved around a lot when I was growing up. I don't know how many places we fixed before packing up again. This isn't anything I haven't done before."

But it was all work she'd never done *alone* before.

Nick's eyebrows rose, but instead of the doubt she expected to see, his dark gaze reflected admiration and a touch of...wariness. "That's a lot to do by yourself."

Ignoring her own doubts, Darcy insisted, "I can handle it."

"Speaking of handling things, I saw the found dog poster you put up. You got more than you bargained for by taking in a stray, didn't you?"

"I wasn't expecting a houseful of puppies." She'd thought for sure she would have heard from the owner by now, but if that call didn't come, it was going to be up to her to see they found good homes.

"Why do you do that?"

Nick's question checked Darcy's reflex action of reaching for her shoulder. She instantly lowered her arm, but the catch on her watch snagged on the material, pulling the collar aside. His gaze locked on the scars, and Darcy couldn't help feeling a little exposed, her childhood fears on display for all to see.

"It's nothing," she said dismissively. "When I was a kid, I was over at a classmate's house. They started roughhousing with their dog, playing keep-away with one of those rope toys."

It had all seemed like such a game when the older boys dangled the twisted rope out of reach and the dog leaped into the air, its snapping jaws just missing the toy. Darcy still wasn't sure when the mood had changed, when the teasing turned into taunting and the dog turned from playful to frustrated. But when one of the boys overthrew his friend and the rope sailed toward her, she'd automatically reached out and caught it.

"Then next thing I knew, the dog was charging right at me. I pulled back my arm to try to throw the rope away, but it was too late. The dog grabbed at it—"

"And caught you instead."

"It was an accident. I know that now, but at the time, I was terrified. I'm still a little afraid."

"You should have said something."

Remembering he hadn't been too quick to believe her when she had said the dog wasn't hers, Darcy asked, "Would it have mattered?"

"Maybe. Maybe not," he confessed. His honesty, even when it cast him in a poor light, struck something inside Darcy.

One of the good guys, she thought again.

"Taking in the dog was really brave."

Brave would mean overcoming her fear entirely. She'd seen toddlers climbing over enormous dogs who bathed their faces with tongues the size of dish rags, yet she couldn't wipe away her nervousness around a six-pound poodle. She had always downplayed her phobia, doing her best to ignore it, so why on earth had she told Nick?

Shaking off the question, she fell back into familiar territory. "Anyway, it was a long time ago. I hardly ever think about it anymore."

"Right."

Darcy heard the doubt in Nick's voice, only then realizing she'd reached up to her collarbone once more. Frustrated by the telltale action, she pretended to adjust her shirt. Only somehow Nick's hand got in the way, and Darcy froze, her gaze locked on his as he brushed his fingers over the pale reminders.

Her heart thundered at the gentle touch, and she swallowed hard, trying to steel herself against the rush of desire threatening to leave her weak and breathless. "I try to keep them covered."

"Why?"

Thinking the answer obvious, and confused by the puzzled expression on Nick's handsome face, Darcy gave a short laugh. "So no one can see them."

More than once, Aaron had expressed his disappointment that she couldn't wear the strapless and off-the-shoulder cocktail dresses he preferred.

His dark eyes knowing, Nick stated, "They're scars, Darcy. Everyone has them—whether you can see them or not."

And Darcy was pretty sure she'd witnessed some of his earlier as he'd watched his daughter dart away from him, braids flying behind her, to disappear into The Hope Chest without a backward glance. The undisguised love and concern written on his face had told Darcy more than she maybe wanted to know. Whatever had happened between Nick and his ex-wife, the divorce had not been his idea. Darcy had the feeling he would have done anything to keep his family together.

Almost as if he'd read her mind, Nick backed toward the doorway. "I should go. Maddie's waiting for me, probably wondering where I am."

"I saw you two earlier outside the ice cream shop. Looked like Maddie was enjoying her cone."

He shrugged. "Lately, it doesn't seem like she enjoys doing much of anything."

"I'm sure that's not true."

"Yeah, it is. But I keep telling myself it's normal, right? I mean, how much did you enjoy hanging out with your old man when you were a kid?"

"I think I might have," Darcy murmured, relieved not to hear any of the wistful longing that had wandered restlessly through the empty spot in her life. A place she'd never had a father to fill.

Shoving the old ache away, she added, "Growing up it was just me and my mom."

His dark eyes probed hers, seeing more than she wanted to reveal. Was that leftover loneliness and longing from her childhood written on her face for him to see? Could he tell how often she'd wondered what her father would think of her if he had bothered to stick around? Did he ever regret walking away from her, walking away from her mother, to protect his "real" family?

"And look how you turned out," Nick said finally, his tone impossible to read.

From another man, the words might have sounded like a come-on. From Aaron, ambiguity would have hovered like smoke around the open-ended comment, leaving Darcy to try to figure out if it'd been a compliment or an insult.

"Sometimes I wonder..." Tension tightened Nick's features, muscles flexing in his jaw, and revealing the unspo-ken turmoil in the words he left hanging.

A wave of embarrassment washed over Darcy. Was she truly so wrapped up in insecurities from the past that she'd failed to recognize *Nick's* worry in the here and now? A single dad who had custody of his daughter… He had to wonder if he was doing the best job he could, playing both roles and questioning, as any true father would, if his daughter needed the female presence she lacked.

"She's lucky to have you." Reaching out, Darcy touched his arm. An instant flinch of warm, male muscle beneath her hand had her sucking in a quick breath. The reminder of the attraction—*unwanted* attraction—between them sent a slow bloom of heat unfurling from her center even as her fingers slid away. "She is, Nick."

But the tension in his backbone, his shoulders, his jaw, only seemed to grow, and she sensed his recoil as if she were questioning his ability as a father rather than reas-suring him. "Maddie means everything to me. She's my first priority. My only priority."

His single-minded dedication seemed a bit…unhealthy. She opened her mouth only to snap it shut just as quickly. Who was she to give advice? Especially not words of wis-dom about maintaining a balance between owning a suc-cessful business, raising his daughter as a single father *and* finding time to cultivate a healthy relationship.

"I can tell how much you love her."

He took a deep breath. "That's why last night when you…"

His voice trailed off and apology or not, she couldn't resist filling in his thought. "Offered you coffee?"

He closed his eyes, but when his lashes lifted, the heat in his dark eyes burned away her lighthearted teasing. "Yeah, you offered me coffee, but I wanted something more."

Those petals of heat unfurled inside her once more. Somehow she didn't think he was talking about espresso, although from the sudden jolt dancing through her veins, she might have already had three shots of the stuff.

But hadn't Nick just gotten through telling her how his time and energy was strictly for his daughter? Whatever *more* was he looking for, she couldn't shake the feeling it would somehow be so much less than what she wanted.

"I think, maybe, we might both be better off if we were just—"

"Caffeine free?" he suggested, that wry flash of humor making him so much harder to resist, and Darcy had the feeling, when it came to Nick Pirelli, if she wasn't careful, she could become completely, hopelessly addicted.

And that wouldn't do. Not at all.

Stepping out of Darcy's shop, Nick couldn't help feeling he'd just made an unlikely escape. It hardly mattered that he hadn't been caught by anything more dangerous than Darcy's easy smile or the featherlight touch of her hand. Logical or not, adrenaline from a close call pulsed through him as he headed toward The Hope Chest. But beneath it all was the awareness that this was only a temporary reprieve. Because a big part of him had wanted to stay right where he was, within Darcy's reach, held captive by the possibilities between them.

The possibility of a kiss, a touch, of holding Darcy in his arms. That was the "more" he'd wanted in Darcy's kitchen, the "more" he still wanted now, and he didn't know how long he'd be able to deny it.

Lost in thought he nearly ran into Marlene Leary. Good manners dictated offering an apology, but the words practically stuck in his throat as he tried stepping past the well-dressed, older woman.

He should have known it wouldn't be so easy. Though his family and the Learys were bound to cross paths in a town so small, Marlene's scowling presence was more than a coincidence.

"I would think, Mr. Pirelli," she said, her chilly gaze aimed at Darcy's shop, "that a man in your circumstances would take care to be more…particular about the company he keeps."

Nick gritted his teeth with the effort it took to keep from telling the snobbish, hypocritical woman what she could do with her advice. The Learys had long held a grudge against his family—one that was totally undeserved. After all, five years ago it had been their daughter, Amy, who had broken in and vandalized Hope Daniels's shop and then allowed Sophia to take the blame. Her recent move back home had Marlene's panties twisted up good. No doubt the woman would have her pointed nose stuck in all their business from now on.

But, even knowing all that, Nick couldn't get around the aggravating fact that she was right. If he were single, nothing would stop him from taking the chance to explore the desire between him and Darcy, to see where it might lead and enjoy a few "meaningless dates" of their own.

As a single father, though, he *did* have to be particular. He had a woman in mind, the right kind of woman this time, and no matter what his hormones thought, that woman was not Darcy Dawson.

Chapter Six

To the Pirellis, nothing was more important than family. That bond had held them together through thick and thin, and Nick counted on his parents and his siblings in ways he wouldn't dream of depending on the best of friends.

Friends come and go, his mother had once told him after some meaningless fight he'd had with Sam, *but family is forever.*

In his heart, Nick believed that to be true which had made the end of his marriage—something else he'd believed would last forever—so hard to take. It had also given him an even greater appreciation for his family who had helped him out in countless ways after Carol's desertion.

He'd never be able to repay that or even get his parents to admit he owed them, but one thing Nick could do was to show up for family dinners. His mother strictly refused her children's offers to hold these dinners someplace other than Vanessa and Vince's home. But Nick made a habit to always bring something—flowers for the table, a bottle of wine, dessert. Which meant dinners at his parents' house were often preceded by trips to the local bakery.

The bell above the door to Bonnie's Bakery rang, and as usual, Nick thought the shop smelled like heaven on earth. Glass displays on either side of the checkout counter were filled with cookies and cakes and cupcakes in every flavor imaginable. Arranged on lace doilies and surrounded by flower arrangements, the desserts looked as good as they tasted.

"Nick." Debbie Mattson stepped out from the back of the shop and greeted him with a dimpled smile. "I was wondering if I'd be seeing you soon. I take it you're here to order your regular?"

He nodded. "Chocolate on chocolate." As his father liked to say, you don't mess with the best, and everyone vowed Debbie's moist chocolate fudge cake was the best.

"When did you want to pick it up?"

"Next Friday. Maddie and I will stop by here on the way to my parents' house."

As Debbie wrote on an order form sitting next to the register, she asked, "How's Maddie doing? Is she looking forward to getting back to school?"

"It's kind of tough to tell what she's thinking lately," Nick admitted.

But *he* was counting the days until the school year started. Not because he wanted his daughter out of his hair, but because he still couldn't shake the feeling that his ex was up to something. She'd been a little too accommodating lately—calling at agreed-upon times, taking a few minutes to talk to him before asking to speak with Maddie.

Carol was never that agreeable unless she wanted something. But whatever she was planning, she was running out of time. Once Maddie was back in school, she couldn't go on any trips. And Nick could breathe easy….at least until fall break rolled around.

"Well, she has to be excited about being Sophia's flower girl," Debbie was saying. "Speaking of the wedding, I was wondering if you'd be able to do me a favor and taste test some wedding cakes."

"Shouldn't that be up to the bride and groom?"

"And Sophia and Jake will taste the cake—as soon as I can narrow down the choices. Sophia has a wedding dress to fit into and I know she feels a little self-conscious being a pregnant bride. She doesn't need to sample two dozen cakes just because I love them all."

"I'm sure she's already said so, but I know how much the work you're doing for her wedding means to Sophia, and the whole family is grateful for the way you've welcomed her back home."

After the break-in at Hope Daniels's shop and the blame that had fallen on Sophia, his sister had been reluctant to return to her hometown. But Debbie had embraced his sister, never having believed the Learys' version of the break-in.

"I'm just glad she's back. She's a Clearville girl. This is where she belongs."

"You're right about that." He shouldn't have been surprised that Debbie shared his view. After all, she was a Clearville girl, too. "So, two dozen cakes, huh? I didn't know there even were that many kinds."

"It's not just the cake. It's the combination of frosting and filling and layers and—" Cutting herself off, she said, "Wait here," before disappearing into the back of the bakery. After a few minutes, she returned with a silver platter balanced in her hands. Thinly sliced pieces of cake rested on individual plates. "I talk too much as it is. Time to let the cakes speak for themselves."

She didn't have to ask him twice. The first piece to catch

his eye was, not surprisingly, a rich chocolate with a raspberry filling. One bite of the decadent chocolate and tart berries was enough to make him think he'd died and gone to dessert heaven. "That's it," he said, knowing the only way Debbie could possibly top it was if she pulled a gallon of milk from her apron. "That's the one."

She grinned but pushed another piece his way. "You can't make a fair decision until you try them all."

He tried three more—a white cake with what Debbie told him was a lemon curd filling, an angel food with banana-strawberry cream and a carrot cake with cream cheese frosting. The last was white with a dusting of coconut like snow on a winter's day.

Still thinking the chocolate raspberry couldn't be beat, Nick stabbed a small piece with the fork and took a bite. Then another. And another. The coconut with just a hint of pineapple melted on his taste buds and created a kind of craving that a bite or two would never satisfy. "This... this is amazing."

"Better than chocolate?" Debbie teased.

"Better than—"

Sex.

The expression was one he'd never understood because, well, come on. But as the thought filtered through his mind, he knew why the tropical flavors had stirred something inside—a hunger he couldn't satisfy because it had nothing to do with cake.

"I know it's a departure from the typical wedding cake," Debbie was saying, "but it's my take on a piña colada."

"It's, um, amazing."

"Really? Because for a second there, you didn't seem so sure."

Maybe because during that second, memories of the almost kiss in Darcy's kitchen had assailed him so strongly, he would have sworn she was once more standing next to him, only a hairsbreadth away. "It's incredible, Debbie, really. Just unexpected."

Though, much to Nick's frustration, it probably shouldn't have been. He'd already learned over the past week that out of sight wasn't out of mind when it came to the gorgeous redhead. He couldn't drive by her shop without glancing through the front window, hoping to catch a glimpse of her. Like Debbie's bite-size cakes, those quick passes simply left him wanting more.

"So, you think it's the one?"

He looked down at the tiny plate he'd scraped spotless with the edge of the plastic fork and felt his face start to heat. If Debbie hadn't been standing on the opposite side of the counter, he probably would have licked the plate clean. "Actually, no. Don't get me wrong, it's my favorite."

"I noticed," the baker said with a cheeky smile.

"But it's—well, it's not right for a wedding. It's too unusual, too…exotic. I think you're better off going with something more—"

"Boring?"

"I was going to say traditional," he argued, feeling a little defensive and wondering if he was even still talking about wedding cakes. "Nothing you make is boring, and both the chocolate and strawberry-banana were great."

"I knew I could count on you, Nick."

"Oh, yeah, you can always count on me to eat whatever you make."

"No, not just that." Debbie eyed him thoughtfully. "When I try something new or different, most people around here will tell me it's 'good' or 'fine' even if they hate it. But you—you don't sugarcoat your opinion."

"Is that another way of saying I'm rude?" he asked wryly. Carol had peppered almost every conversation during their marriage with questions that had no right answers, and she'd told him on more than one occasion that he was too brusque, too sharp, too rough around the edges.

"No, not rude. Honest. Unfailingly honest." Debbie grinned. "I like that about you, Nick."

As he half listened to Debbie talk about her plans for Sophia and Jake's wedding cake, Nick realized there was a lot to like about Debbie, too. She was Clearville born and raised—just like he was. She had deep roots in the town and ran her own business—just like he did. In fact, Debbie had been working at her family's bakery since she was a little kid, then taking over more and more of the duties while she was still in high school when her mother fell ill.

She was smart and funny and kind. That she baked like a dream went without saying, and she was good with children, too. Nick had been in her shop enough times to see the bite-size cookies she kept on hand to pass out to any kids who crossed her threshold. She wasn't model thin like Carol and didn't have Darcy's elegant curves, but Debbie had always been comfortable with her full figure, and with her blond curls and blue eyes, she was very pretty.

How had he never noticed that before?

"Anyway, I— Nick, are you okay? You just had the strangest expression on your face."

"Fine, yes. Sure."

Debbie could be the right woman—the one he and Maddie needed. With the baker staring at him quizzically, Nick waited for…something. A spark, a flicker, a hint of attraction. But other than the fondness he'd always felt, there was nothing.

A wave of disappointment washed over him followed by a faint undertow that almost felt like…relief. He could still sense Debbie watching though the plate-glass window after they had said their goodbyes and he left the bakery.

She was a great girl. Everything he thought he wanted. And yet… Was it wrong of him to want something more?

Irritated, Nick started walking as if he could march his thoughts into submission. Hadn't he learned his lesson with Carol? He'd fallen hard for her and landed even harder. That sudden breath-stealing desire—the kind he felt for Darcy—didn't last.

And even though he'd watched her from a distance this past week, as she worked long hours to remodel the shop on her own, just as she had said she would, he couldn't forget what she'd already told him.

This was the kind of thing she'd done her whole life—fixing a place up before moving on. And while that abandoned, empty space she'd rented might be in better shape by the time she packed up and left, if he let her into his life, into the abandoned, empty space in his heart, he damn well wouldn't be able to say the same.

Standing in the middle of her shop, Darcy stared at the shades of dirt on the carpet and wondered where to begin. She supposed at one time, the carpeting had an actual pattern, but between being faded and worn and stained, the whole thing was now an indistinguishable mess. Unfortunately, removing it was going to be an even bigger mess, but she had little choice. No way was she opening her shop with this carpeting down on these floors.

Early morning sunlight streamed through the floor-to-ceiling windows she'd washed and dried and then washed some more until not a water spot or streak remained. The previous weekend's storm had blown away the clouds and fog that occasionally rolled in and out with the tide, and she had the front door open to welcome in the fresh, clean air. She'd come prepared, bringing her tools with her along with safety goggles and a mask.

A must for summer accessories, she thought with a smile, and the perfect way to complete her working wardrobe of worn, paint-splattered jeans and faded blue tank top.

She'd meant every word when she had told Nick Pirelli she wasn't afraid to get dirty, and it was time to prove it.

Not to him, of course, Darcy thought as she picked a threadbare spot in the corner to start peeling back the carpet. She and her mother had carried this dream through every move they'd made for the past two decades. Really, it had nothing at all to do with the oh-so-serious vet who'd never dreamed a day in his life. Nothing to do with proving her shop wouldn't be one of those places that had a going-out-of-business sale before the grand opening signs came down. Nothing to do with showing him that she wasn't some city girl who would hightail it back to "civilization" the first time she couldn't find the latest fashions in Clearville.

Nothing to do with him at all.

But Darcy had to admit the "more" Nick spoke about wanting had crept into her thoughts on an almost embarrassingly regular basis, along with a few fantasies of just what that simple word might mean. She'd done the right thing in refusing his vague offer, if he'd even intended his comment as some kind of proposition, but like anyone quitting caffeine cold turkey, the more she told herself she couldn't have it, the more she craved it.

And she couldn't help thinking that "more," no matter how much less it might be than she wanted, was still better than the nothing she had now.

A broad-shouldered shadow passed over the wall in front of her a second before Darcy heard the scrape of a boot against the doorjamb. Her pulse danced a happy beat until she glanced over her shoulder.

Daydreaming about Nick Pirelli, it turned out, was not enough to make the man appear. Rising to her feet, she faced Travis Parker. She pushed her safety goggles onto the top of her head but kept the hammer in hand as she asked, "What are you doing here, Travis?"

The sandy-haired man grinned, cockiness backing his stride as he sauntered in as if she'd welcomed him with open arms. "You haven't returned my calls."

Which a smarter man would recognize as a woman's desire *not* to talk to him again. "I've been busy getting my shop ready."

"So I see."

Only he wasn't looking at her shop. Refusing to squirm beneath his overly interested stare, she said, "Then you can see how busy I am. I don't have time—"

"All the more reason for me to lend a hand. So you and I will have time."

She shook her head. Some guys just didn't get it. And if she allowed him to take another two steps closer, Darcy had a good idea his "helping" hands would be following the path his eyes had already taken.

"Thanks for the offer, Travis…"

Anyone else would have heard the "but" coming next from a mile away. Not Travis. "You are more than welcome," he said over her unspoken protest as he sidled closer.

His charmer's grin was firmly in place, but Darcy wondered if the man wasn't used to hearing the word *no* or if he purposely ignored women when they said it. "And don't you worry about payment. We can work something out together."

The night Nick had answered her emergency call, she'd teased him about bartering for services, hoping to crack through his stiff exterior and to see him relax into a smile.

But with Travis, Darcy didn't feel like joking, and his smile was making her skin crawl.

"Like I was saying, thank you—but no thank you. I'm not looking for help—"

"Darcy already has all the help she needs."

The no-nonsense words came from the doorway, and a shiver of awareness raced down her spine. Even with Travis blocking her line of sight, Darcy recognized the deep voice. So, too, did Travis if the tightening of his jaw and puffed-out chest were anything to go by. Turning to face the other man, he said, "Didn't know you were in the handyman business, Doc."

"I'm not. But my brother runs one of the most successful contracting companies around. You know that, Parker."

Darcy might not have understood the history behind it, but she recognized the dig in Nick's words as easily as Travis did. The other man's hands fisted at his sides. "This isn't the kind of job Drew takes on."

"He would for friends of the family."

Friends. Darcy didn't know exactly what to make of that, but the friends-of-the-Pirellis tag Nick bestowed upon her seemed to do the trick. Travis shot her a final, disgruntled look before striding toward the door. A brief, silent battle of wills took place as he and Nick stood toe to toe, but when the vet refused to give ground, Travis circled around and stormed out onto the sidewalk.

Exhaling a sigh of relief, Darcy said, "Thank you. I could have handled it myself—"

"Yeah, I bet you could." Nick stepped closer and reached out. Only when his fingers closed around her wrist and lifted her arm did she realize she still held the hammer. "I'm almost sorry I didn't get to see you use this."

Giving a slightly embarrassed laugh, she set aside the

tool on the worn checkout counter. "Travis doesn't understand subtle hints."

"Hmm, guess maybe those meaningless dates of yours meant more to him than they did to you."

Darcy opened her mouth to argue, but the words stuck in her throat. After all, she had said they'd been meaningless dates, but that didn't mean *all* her dates were meaningless. A date with Nick… That would mean way too much if her rapidly pounding heart was anything to go by.

"Something tells me Travis will live to harass another day."

"Do you have to ward off all your former dates with hammers?"

"No. Sometimes I break out the power tools."

Darcy wasn't sure which of them was more startled by Nick's sudden bark of laughter, but the deep, unexpected sound settled deep in her belly, tumbling and turning and encouraging her to join in.

She wasn't sure when laughter faded into silence…. When the nerves in her stomach trembled with something so much more potent… When the spark in his eyes caught fire…

"Nick."

His name was a mere whisper of sound, but it captured his full attention. His gaze dropped to her mouth, and she ran her tongue over her lower lip as if she could already taste him there. Her pulse pounded through her veins, and Darcy realized this was no caffeine addiction. Her need for Nick went so much deeper than that. Straight to her heart, she feared, and if he didn't kiss her… If he didn't kiss her now…

The echo of his name was still on her lips when his mouth claimed hers. His body trapped her against the counter, only she didn't feel the need to escape. She couldn't imagine any other place she wanted to be.

The room spun in circles and the morning light filling the shop dimmed into intimate shadows. Caught up in his kiss, Darcy didn't realize it wasn't only the brush of his lips, the tempting stroke of his tongue, the heat and strength of his body making her head whirl. Only when she felt the wall at her back did she figure out that those slightly dizzying turns had been Nick guiding them into the small hallway at the back of the shop, out of view from the plate-glass windows.

Not total privacy, not enough privacy, but she would take what she could get. She would take whatever Nick would give. He must have sensed her thoughts as he angled his head, deepening the kiss, and pressed his body's full length to hers. Her knees trembled, but with the wall at her back and Nick in front of her, her bones could have melted into wax and she wouldn't have moved. Didn't want to move.

She fisted her hands in the back of his shirt, soft cotton warmed by the heat of his skin, and tugged, wanting to feel that heat, that skin free of any barriers. She whispered his name as his lips burned a trail down her throat, but it was another sound—the faint tinkling of the bell over her door—that had them both freezing.

Holding her breath, Darcy tried to hear over the pulse still pounding in her ears. But there was nothing. No sound of footsteps, no curious hello. "Must have been the wind," she said, but Nick had already pulled away.

He tucked in his shirt, smoothed his hands through his hair, erasing all signs of what just happened before he finally met her gaze. "Darcy—"

She read the regret in his expression and pressed her fingers to his lips. Disappointment doused the passion, the excitement, the perfection of the past few moments. "I know what you're going to say," she whispered, her voice still husky with those lingering feelings. "I've heard it all before."

She didn't need the words when his withdrawal had already fractured her heart just a bit. Not so much that it wouldn't heal, but enough for her to know where she was headed if she didn't end this, if she didn't let him walk away now.

But how could she when kissing him, talking to him, simply breathing the same air he did, felt so *right?* It sounded crazy, but like the first time she drove down Main Street, seeing images from books and magazines and internet pages brought to life around her, she knew she'd found what she'd spent her whole life hoping to find. Clearville was home. And Nick was...

She shied away from where her thoughts were heading, not yet ready to define what he could be. But words like *affair* and *fling* didn't come close to describing the rush of emotion she experienced in his arms. Not for her and— she was betting her heart on this—not for Nick, either. He wasn't a player like Travis Parker, out for whatever action he could get. So it had to mean something, didn't it, for a man as controlled as Nick to lose that control, to kiss her with such heat and hunger?

Taking a risk, she trailed her fingertips from his lips, down his throat to his chest where his heart still pounded as crazily as hers did. Heat flared in his eyes and an answering flush bloomed in her cheeks. "Maybe instead of worrying about what this thing between us can or can't be, we should focus on what it is."

A muscle worked in his jaw as if trying to hold back the words he couldn't stop himself from asking. "And what exactly is it?"

"I'd have to say it's pretty much...irresistible."

* * *

"You okay, Doc?"

Looking away from the computer to the open door-way to his office, Nick forced himself to meet his assistant's gaze. He'd been staring at the screen, pretending to be working more than actually getting anything done, but Rhonda wasn't one to be easily fooled. The attractive forty-something widow had worked for decades for the vet whose practice Nick took over when the older man retired. She was sharp and sassy and would sense anything unusual going on, anything out of the ordinary.

Like kissing Darcy Dawson.

Couldn't get any more unusual or extraordinary than that. The logical part of him still couldn't believe he'd kissed her even though the rest of him had no doubt. The taste of her lips, the silken feel of her hair pouring through his fingers, the curves of her body pressed against him—

"Um, Doc?"

Blinking, Nick realized his assistant was still waiting on his answer and he had little chance of convincing her it was just another day. "What is it, Rhon?"

"I thought we agreed I make a lousy cup of coffee."

The out-of-the-blue comment threw him, but not so much that he didn't answer honestly. "You do."

"In that case, here's a lousy cup of coffee and the mes-sages off the machine." Arching her eyebrows above her dark-framed glasses, she crossed the room, clunked a steaming mug onto his desk and held up a stack of pa-pers. Two things he always, always did after opening the office were taking the messages off voice mail and start-ing the coffee in the tiny break room. "You okay, Doc?" she repeated.

Nick didn't even know where to begin to answer that question. Too bad Darcy hadn't used that hammer on him.

Maybe it would have knocked some sense into his thick skull. "Fine. Thanks," he added as he took the notes from her hand.

"Everything all right with Maddie?"

The simple question sent guilt slamming into his gut. Rhonda had been thinking about his daughter when Nick's own thoughts had been solely focused on what he wanted. On the woman he wanted.

He mumbled a reassurance at his assistant, who seemed to think twice about pressing him for details and left him alone instead. Maddie was fine; he knew that. He'd dropped her off at summer camp that morning and she'd eagerly raced off to join her friends.

But hadn't he decided if he was going to let a woman in his life, into their lives, it would be the right kind of woman this time? That he would follow his head, not his heart…and for damn sure not the hormones raging through his body.

Swearing beneath his breath, he eyed the phone situated on the corner of his desk. He had many of the local businesses programmed into the system, including the number for Bonnie's Bakery. One push of a button, and he could move forward with his plan.

But his hand refused to reach for the keypad even as he reminded himself of all the qualities that made Debbie the perfect woman. She was pretty, kind, funny. She was Clearville born and raised and had deep roots, professional and personal, in the town they both loved.

For all of that, and a dozen other pros in her favor, the one item on the con list had him turning away from the phone with a frustrated sigh.

She wasn't Darcy.

Until he could shake this ridiculous fascination with Darcy Dawson, he didn't have a snowball's chance of focusing on anyone else. And yet hadn't he felt more alive and aware when he was with Darcy than he had in months? Years? He felt as though he'd been moving on autopilot, doing what needed to be done with little sense of anticipation or fulfillment. But with Darcy... It was like a change from running on dim, dying batteries to plugging into 120 volts. Everything around him seemed so much more vivid, focused and energized.

Irresistible... Was Darcy right? Was that instant, elemental attraction between them leading down an inevitable road? And did he really have to resist?

If he cut loose this once, if he let himself have a bit of fun for now, would it really change his mind about his long-term goal? Or might it instead be a chance to get Darcy out of his system so he could move on?

He took a swallow from the mug, but the dark brew just made him feel a little sicker to his stomach, and not simply because Rhonda's coffee really was lousy. He wasn't the type to use women for his own purposes and cast them aside. Those games were for SOBs like Travis Parker.

Of course, it didn't seem like Darcy was suffering any from her brief fling with Love 'Em and Leave 'Em Travis. If anything, roles had reversed and Travis was the one coming back for more. Something Nick would have considered just deserts if not for the protective and possessive desire to keep the man away from Darcy.

Darcy, who'd made it more than plain she could take care of herself. And who'd been on more dates in her two months in Clearville than Nick had been on during an entire year. So was he *really* worried that she might end up falling for him?

Yeah, right. Jeez, could he be a bigger idiot?

But maybe Darcy was right. Maybe this attraction between them was a detour they could explore together.

Chapter Seven

"So what do you think, Doc?"

Nick joined Jarrett Deeks at the corral fence. The other man stood with his arms crossed on the top rail as he looked out over half-a-dozen trail horses. His straw cowboy hat was pulled low over his dark hair, shading his expression, though with the clouds rolling in off the ocean some miles away, he didn't really need it.

Beyond his time in the rodeo and his love of horses, Nick knew very little about Jarrett Deeks. He was certainly a man who kept his thoughts and opinions to himself, but Nick didn't think he was telling the cowboy anything he didn't already know when he said, "He looks great, Jarrett. Better than I would have hoped."

Thanks to Jarrett's efforts, the rescue horse he'd taken in a few weeks ago had put on weight. The shine was back on his gray coat, and as Nick watched, the horse tossed its head and took a spirited gallop across the corral. The change was remarkable, and he couldn't help grinning. "It's amazing."

The brim of the cowboy hat dipped in response to Nick's words. Jarrett played things pretty close to the vest, but his lips curved into a smile his hat couldn't hide. "I can't take credit, though. She deserves all the thanks."

"She?" As Nick echoed the word, he followed the other man's gaze to a small chestnut mare. He watched as the rescue horse trotted over and nudged the other horse with its nose.

"I was keeping him away from the rest of the horses at first. He was so weak. But even after he started regaining his strength, something was missing. That spark, you know? And all it took was putting the two of them together."

A spark. A flicker of interest. A buzz of excitement. A rush of attraction...

Hell, he'd been missing it way too long himself, but now that he'd found it—now that he'd found Darcy—he didn't have a clue what to do. Shelving his plan to find a woman to settle down with had been the first step. He had no respect for men who had a wife or girlfriend at home and another woman on the side. If he was going to pursue this thing with Darcy, then that was what he would do.

Jump into the fire until the flame died down without making the mistake of thinking that kind of heat could last.

Jarrett glanced at his watch, then over at a dirt road that led back behind the stables and disappeared into a row of pine trees flirting with the low-hanging clouds. The wind picked up, combing through the horses' tails, and Nick figured he'd be lucky to make it down the mountain road before the storm hit.

"You don't still have riders on the trails, do you?" Weekend wannabe cowboys who'd watched too many Clint Eastwood westerns wouldn't enjoy getting in touch with Mother Nature when her sun wasn't shining.

The other man heaved a sigh somewhere between annoyance and self-deprecation. "There's someone out there, but she's not on the trails or on horseback."

Thunder rolled a low warning, adding to Nick's bad-luck feeling. "Not on the trails…"

"I'm pretty sure the city girl doesn't ride."

City girl…

"Let me guess," he said grimly. "Tall, curvy, long red hair."

"You got her."

"What the hell is Darcy Dawson doing out there?"

Jarrett raised a lean shoulder in a shrug. "Beats me. She came out here a couple hours ago, all fired up to go see the Whiteside farmhouse. Or what used to be the farmhouse since the place has been empty for decades."

"I thought you would have torn it down by now," Nick murmured, still baffled by why Darcy would be driving around to see abandoned farmland.

"That's part of the plan. Just haven't gotten around to it."

When Jarrett had first moved to Clearville and began buying up land for his stables, Nick had heard plans to add a few cabins, maybe even turn the place into a dude ranch. None of that talk came from Jarrett, though, so he figured the stories were simply the Clearville grapevine getting tangled up again.

None of which explained what Darcy was doing out there.

A fork of lightning streaked down in the distance, and Jarrett said, "I've gotta get the horses inside. If she's not back by then—"

"I'll go look for her," Nick interrupted. He wouldn't be able to stop wondering what she was doing, so he might as well have something productive to do while he was thinking it.

"You sure?" At Nick's nod, Jarrett waved his thanks and opened the fence to round up the horses.

Climbing back into his SUV and eyeing the darkening sky, Nick recalled his last visit to Jarrett's ranch and the call that had taken him to Darcy's house. At the time, he'd half suspected she'd fabricated the emergency. Now, he found himself hoping he was the one jumping the gun.

He'd only driven a few miles over the uneven, pitted dirt road when the skies opened up. Windshield wipers swept back and forth in a quick rhythm, but so much rain coated the glass, he felt like he was driving underwater. The towering pines on either side bowed and swayed to the force of the storm. He swore when he hit a pothole hard enough to bounce him off his seat. The steering wheel jerked in his hands, and anger started burning inside him, cauterizing the fear he didn't want to face.

Mountain roads were nothing to mess with. Not on good days. Not on the *paved* roads.

Finally, through the watery blur of the windshield, he caught sight of a flash of red on the side of the road—Darcy's small sedan. His SUV slid to a muddy stop as he reached for the door. The wind nearly ripped the handle from his hand, and he squinted against the slash of rain in his face. He was soaked almost the instant he stepped outside. But that was nothing compared to Darcy who stood at the back of her car, trying—he suspected—to wedge something beneath the sunken back tire. Judging by the tilt of the vehicle, it was going to take more than that to pull the car free of the mud.

Her hair streaming down her back and rain dripping from her face, she met his gaze over the roof of her car. Relief seemed to war with resignation in her green gaze as she raced to the passenger side of his SUV. Raising her voice over the pounding rain all around them, she said, "I was trying—"

Cutting her off with an abrupt "Get in," he didn't wait for her to move. Especially not after an angry crack overhead followed a violent gust of wind. Scooping her into his arms, he dropped her onto the SUV's passenger's seat before circling the hood and climbing behind the wheel. Slamming the door shut, he demanded, "What the hell were you doing out here?"

Probably not the best conversation starter with a woman he'd wanted to take to bed, but dammit, he wanted to know what she'd been thinking!

Darcy stiffened, clearly annoyed by his tone, and crossed her arms over the long-sleeved, blue T-shirt she wore. The dark color didn't disappear into transparency the way a lighter material would have, but between the rain and the cold, it didn't take much imagination to picture the shape and the size of her breasts.

The softness of her skin, though… That was still worth imagining.

"Gee, Nick, I don't know. I guess it seemed like a nice day for a drive."

His hands tightened on the wheel as he backed into the brush on the side of the road and turned around. She'd win points for attitude, no doubt about that, but the delivery, given through chattering teeth, dimmed the smart-ass effect. Cranking up the heat, he aimed the vents in her direction. "Take off your shirt."

Peering through the heavy rain, he couldn't risk taking his eyes from the road, but he still caught a sideways glimpse of her head whipping in his direction. "Excuse me?"

He bit back a comment about going topless on such a

"nice day" and instead said, "You're freezing, and there's a shirt in the backseat. You'll warm up a lot faster without the wet clothes on."

As she twisted around, her damp hair brushed his arm, sending a shiver of desire racing down his spine. "What about you?" she asked as she pulled the denim shirt onto her lap.

Just the thought of Darcy taking off her clothes heated his blood to the point where he half expected steam to start rising from his skin. "I'll be fine."

In the interest of their safety—and his sanity—he kept his gaze fixed straight ahead as she peeled the wet T-shirt over her head. But even with that serious effort, he still had the vision of pale skin, naked shoulders and firm breasts covered by baby-blue silk taunting him. With his shirt finally in place, she rubbed her hands up and down her arms, her chills gradually subsiding.

But he had a good idea she was still shaken by what had happened when they'd been driving on the highway for ten minutes before she asked, "Where are we going?"

"My place is closer. We can dry off there, get something to eat and wait for the storm to die down a bit before I take you home."

Dropping her head back on the rest, she gave a low moan. "What about my car?"

"Was it damaged? Did you run over anything?"

"No, it was just stuck."

"You're lucky it was just stuck. You—"

Darcy shook her head. "Nick, thank you. For the rescue and for the ride, but I don't want to talk about it, okay?"

He took his eyes off the road just long enough to meet her gaze. Her green eyes were snapping beneath her lowered brows, and the heat in the SUV had brought color back to her cheeks. But despite the stubborn, defiant tilt of her jaw, he read the hurt she was trying to hide.

He didn't know why she'd driven out to the middle of nowhere, but whatever she found had broken her heart.

Tucked into the corner of a leather couch in front of a crackling fire, a soft chenille blanket draped over her legs as she waited for a gorgeous dark-haired, dark-eyed man to emerge from the kitchen with something to drink, Darcy thought the entire setting should have embodied enough romance for a jewelry store ad.

Should have…if the gorgeous guy in question wasn't annoyed with her. Again.

But the scowl hadn't left Nick's face since they'd made their mad dash from his SUV into his house. She'd huddled on a small area rug at the front door, trying not to drip on the hardwood floors, as he disappeared down a hallway. He was back a minute later with a towel, yet another shirt for her to change into and a pair of drawstring flannel pajama bottoms. For a second, she thought he might start rubbing her down, like some foolish kid who didn't know when to come in out of the rain, but instead he handed her the bundle in his arms and promised her something to drink once he dried off, too.

His cabin home was small, but every detail was designed with comfort and a love of outdoors in mind—from the river-rock fireplace reaching to the exposed-beam ceiling to the sturdy, man-size furnishings and the wall of windows at the back of the house. Rain streaked the glass leading to a glorious redwood deck with views of the trees and mountains in the distance.

He'd made room for his daughter, too. School photos lined the driftwood mantel, and Darcy spotted some kids' books squeezed in between large volumes on veterinary medicine. A lone pink shoe peeked out from beneath the recliner on the other side of the room, playing hide-and-seek with its mate, and a collection of primary-colored scrunchies decorated the trunk-style coffee table.

Walking in from the kitchen with two steaming mugs in his hands, Nick looked born to the rugged setting. He'd changed clothes as well, into a pair of jeans a little more worn and faded than the last and a long-sleeved green T-shirt.

"I like your place. It suits you."

"Thanks. Drew and I built it together from the ground up."

"That's amazing," she said, looking around with an even greater sense of appreciation, knowing now that Nick had done so much of the work himself. With his own hands.

Darcy swallowed as she thought of Nick's hands on her, and her pulse picked up speed as he drew closer. The awareness of the two of them all alone in this out-of-the-way cabin seemed to fill the split second of silence between every word they spoke.

Handing her one of the mugs, he warned, "Careful. It's hot."

As she wrapped her hands around the warm ceramic, she couldn't help smiling at the unexpected beverage. Hot chocolate with miniature marshmallows bobbing on the creamy surface. Glancing up from beneath her lashes, she caught Nick in a moment of indecision as he eyed the cushion beside her and the recliner a room away.

"Now I get it," she murmured.

"Get what?"

After taking a sip, she lifted the mug in a silent toast. "Wrong drink. Maybe if I'd offered you hot chocolate instead of coffee, you wouldn't have turned me down."

The memory played across his expression like a movie

at an old-time drive-in, and he made up his mind. Dropping a knee onto the cushion beside her, he lowered his body until he was nearly blocking her into her little corner of the couch. "I didn't turn you down."

"'I'm not interested' didn't come across as a resounding yes to me."

Reaching past her, he set his mug on the end table over her shoulder. He was close enough for Darcy to breathe in the rainwater-fresh scent of his damp hair. Close enough to see the long lashes that framed his espresso-dark eyes and the shadow of an afternoon beard lining his rugged jawline and framing the perfection of his lips. He took the mug from her motionless hand to set it aside as well before he murmured her name in a rough whisper "You've caught my interest now."

Memories of their kiss played along her nerve endings, every reminder striking a longing for so much more. "I have?"

"I can't wait to find out," he said as he leaned in, "what you were doing out at the Whiteside farmhouse."

"What?" The word exploded from her in a rush of frustrated desire as Nick leaned back against the couch cushions, crossed his arms over his chest and waited.

Annoyed, she stared back at him. She had to give him credit, though, for playing her better than she'd played him. She could have argued that it was none of his business, could have held her silence. But he had come to her rescue—again—and for that alone, he deserved an explanation. "My grandmother was a Whiteside before she married a Dawson. That was my grandparents' farm. It's where my mother grew up."

Darcy didn't know what she'd expected to find—some piece of her mother, some nostalgic memory of her past. Whatever she'd been looking for, though, she hadn't found it in the run-down, decrepit house that was all that remained of her mother's childhood home. A fallen tree branch had torn through a section of the roof, storm damage had shattered most of the windows and the whole place looked one breath away from blowing down.

She'd tried telling herself it was just a building. A building that held no memories for her. Certainly it no longer held any memories of her mother. But finding it in that condition—broken, abandoned—a feeling of emptiness and loneliness had swept over Darcy.

"It was stupid," she told Nick now. "It's been thirty years since my mother lived in that house. I don't even know what I was looking for."

But Nick seemed to know. His gaze traced over her features, sympathy and understanding written in his dark eyes. "You were looking for a part of your past, trying to connect with your family's history."

And maybe that was why seeing the farmhouse had hurt so much, driving home the painful truth that history—and her memories—were all she had left of her family.

Or at least all she had left of the family she'd been a part of.

The rest of the family—the wealthy businessman who'd never acknowledged her and the siblings who didn't know she existed—they were alive and well. After the way Lawrence Fairchild had abandoned her mother after she became pregnant, Darcy wanted nothing to do with the man. But she'd often wondered about her brother and sister. Make that half brother and half sister, the children her father gladly embraced and posed with for pictures taken at celebrity golf tournaments and charity balls.

How would they react if they found out about her? Given time, would they accept her? Or would they see her only as living proof of their father's infidelity? Contacting them was a risk she'd never taken. After the way Aaron had re-acted when he learned she was her family's dirty little se-cret, she was glad she hadn't found the courage.

She'd been wrong when she thought she could trust Aaron with her most painful secret, and she would think long and hard before opening up like that again.

She stared unblinking into the wavering flames in the fireplace as she willed her tears away, not wanting Nick to see her cry. She was stronger than this. Tougher than this. She wasn't the weak city girl he thought she was, ready to turn tail at the first sign of trouble.

"I keep looking around town, trying to picture her here."

But she couldn't. And yet her mother had talked for years about coming back to Clearville. Owning the bou-tique was Alanna's dream and Darcy felt so disloyal to her mother's memory for doubting she would have made that dream a reality.

Looking up, she met Nick's knowing gaze. "You don't think I belong here, either, do you?"

He hesitated, and her heart skipped a beat, eager to be-lieve she'd changed his mind about her—about *them*. But then Nick shook his head, his jaw tightening to a stubborn and familiar angle. "It doesn't matter what I think."

Oh, but it did! Far more than Darcy wanted to admit. Her desire to settle down, to find a place to call home was changing, growing and expanding right along with the depth of her feelings for the man beside her. It was more than a feel-it-in-her-bones attraction. It was the devotion he showed to his daughter, the love in his voice when he talked about his mother and sister. Even the restraint he'd shown as he kept his eyes on the road when she'd taken off her shirt in the seat next to him, careful not to look though part of her wished he would.

The same needy part of her longed for him to kiss her

now. She was wrapped in his scent, the fresh-laundry smell woven into the clothes she'd borrowed, but it wasn't enough. She wanted to be wrapped in his arms, breathing in the scent from his skin.

"It matters to me," she told him softly. The vulnerability of her confession opened her heart and practically begged him to stomp on it, but she couldn't stop the words from spilling out any more than she could stop her feelings for this man.

"Darcy."

He nearly groaned her name, the tension spreading to the rest of his body, and her heart started to pound. She felt balanced on a razor's edge, knowing no matter what Nick decided, one way or the other, she was headed for a fall.

Tucking her trembling legs beneath her on the cushion, she rose up on her knees and turned his face toward her. Shivers raced up her arm at the faint scrape of his afternoon beard, scattering goose bumps across her chest. "I might not have been born in Clearville, but I was meant to be here."

Meant to be in Clearville. Meant to be here with Nick.

She couldn't explain the certainty that had woven her mother's dream of moving back home and opening the boutique into her own dreams of being with Nick. All she knew was what felt right in her heart. Being with Nick, kissing him, making love with him, all felt inevitable with every moment leading to this one, and she refused to let it slip by.

Some of what she was thinking must have shown on her face because Nick's expression changed. For half a second, she expected him to bolt like he had before. A battle raged, written in his tense features, and Darcy nearly wilted in relief, knowing she'd won when he reached out and pulled her into his arms.

She gasped as she lost her balance, but Nick caught her

as she tumbled into his lap. "You're here now," he murmured between quick, arousing kisses.

"Yes," she gasped as she fisted her hands in the cotton of his shirt.

"That's all that matters."

"Yes."

He pulled her closer, the heat and arousal of his body beneath hers already sending shivers of pleasure through her. "*This* is all that matters."

Pinpricks of doubt threatened that pleasure, but Darcy ignored them. If she admitted she was the one who wanted more, Nick would pull away, and she'd be left with nothing. She'd miss her chance to show him how perfect they would be together. And hadn't she learned to focus on today rather than pinning her hopes on dreams of tomorrow?

Heart pounding in anticipation, she murmured her agreement, hoping she could convince Nick and herself the words were true.

A distant buzz slowly perforated the sensual fog surrounding Nick, breaking through the I-must-be-dreaming daze of making love to Darcy and waking him to the reality of holding her in his arms.

Staring up at the beamed ceiling of his living room, even with the proof of her head resting on his chest, her long red hair trailing over his arm, he could hardly believe what had happened. He'd spent the afternoon making love with Darcy Dawson.

Irresistible. That was how she'd described the attraction between them, not that he'd tried too damn hard to resist. But for a brief second when he'd caught her in his arms, he'd seen something in her green gaze—an uncertainty and vulnerability—and disappointment had slammed into him when he feared she might pull away.

That instant, an almost overwhelming sense of loss had him questioning his own words that the chemistry between them was all that mattered. *Darcy* mattered. Her longing to hold on to the memory of her family. Her determination to make her mother's dream come true. Her laughter, her courage, her compassion, all of that got under his skin, going far deeper than sexual attraction.

But then she'd whispered her answer against his lips, and he'd allowed the surge of desire to silence any lingering doubts.

He didn't know how they stripped away most of their clothes without leaving the couch, but they'd managed amid frantic kisses and hungry caresses. The shirt he'd loaned her was easy enough to remove, and the plain white cotton became the sexiest thing he ever saw as each loosened button revealed more and more fair skin and the inner curves of her breasts.

He groaned, realizing she was naked beneath his clothes, but it wasn't nearly enough. He wanted her naked beneath him. With the shirt still covering her, he reached inside and cupped her soft flesh. She arched her back, seeking more of his touch as his thumbs circled the hard points of her nipples. Her breath came in gasps as she rocked against him, the arousing motion spurring him on.

The flush on her skin and the heat in her eyes beckoned him, and he turned with her on the oversize cushions of the couch. He'd wanted a piece of furniture long enough for him to kick back and stretch out on, but he'd never imagined stretching out with a gorgeous woman beneath him.

He stripped away the drawstring pants and found the feminine heat waiting for him. Her open-mouthed kiss and the faint taste of hot chocolate on her tongue nearly drove him over the edge, but at the last minute, he remembered the condoms he'd bought with Darcy in mind.

She smiled when he returned, protection in hand, a sight sexy enough to stop his heart. "Irresistible," he reminded her when she welcomed him back.

"Yes," she whispered, and then again as he sank inside her. He tried holding back, wanting to prolong the pleasure, feeling it was all too much, too soon. But as Darcy's hips rose and fell with his thrusts and she cried out his name, tremors racking her body, he followed her into an almost unimaginable release.

Irresistible, they'd both agreed. But already it felt like it was so much more...

Gradually Nick's thoughts came back to the present, and he realized the faint tremor wasn't aftershocks from the most amazing sex of his life, but the vibration of his cell phone. A sound he belatedly realized had been going on for some time.

Darcy made a soft sound of protest as he eased away, making it that much harder to leave, but he had to answer his phone. Hell, he had to find his phone, he thought as he picked up his jeans off the floor and found the pockets empty. Swearing beneath his breath, he quickly pulled the jeans on before heading to his bedroom and the damp clothes he'd stripped off earlier.

The phone had stopped vibrating by the time he fished it out of the back pocket, but a much stronger reverberation slammed into his chest when he looked at the screen.

Five missed calls. All from Maddie's summer camp.

Pulse pounding, he redialed the number, immediately talking over the counselor's cheery greeting. "This is Nick Pirelli. Someone's been trying to reach me about my daughter."

"Oh, yes, Dr. Pirelli. Hi. With the bad weather, our field trip to the beach was canceled. Some of the parents picked up their children early, including MaryAnne Martin.

Maddie wanted to go with Rachel—you know what good friends they are—but since we weren't able to reach you for permission, we couldn't allow Maddie to go. She's… rather upset."

A canceled field trip. Not an emergency. Not anything to get worked up over unless you were an eight-year-old girl stuck at camp without your best friend. But that didn't change the load of guilt that dropped down on Nick when he first saw those messages.

"I'm sorry about all the calls," the counselor was saying. "I thought you might be in the middle of some kind of emergency, but up until now, you've always been so good about letting us know who to contact in those situations."

Up until now, he'd never been in this kind of situation. Never spent an afternoon making love to a woman he couldn't get out of his head.

Shoving aside that thought, he told the young woman on the phone, "Let Maddie know I'll be there to pick her up in a half hour." Then slammed shut his phone.

"Is everything okay?"

The quiet question sounded from the doorway, and he couldn't stop himself from turning. Hair rumpled and lips swollen from his kisses, Darcy stood in the hallway wearing the shirt he'd given her. The long sleeves fell to her fingertips and its tails covered her to her knees, longer than a lot of dresses, but the sight lit his blood to a slow boil. Because it was his shirt? Because he'd already taken it off her once? Or because he now knew what was beneath?

"It's fine. Maddie's fine. Camp was cut short due to the storm. I have to go pick her up." He dug through a dresser drawer for another shirt as he spoke. After dragging it on, he searched for his keys and wallet in the jeans he'd worn earlier and transferred them to his pockets.

"Nick." Darcy stepped closer, the soft touch on his arm

slowing his movements. The same touch that had aroused him to such heights minutes ago now had the power to soothe him, to comfort him—if he let her. "Relax. You said everything's okay, right?"

Not even close to okay, he thought as he met the caring and concern in her gaze and finally admitted what he'd refused to see. Darcy wasn't just a city girl with a gorgeous face, amazing body and sexy laugh who could turn his head. She was a smart, strong, sensitive woman who could twist his heart. He hadn't felt so strongly about a woman—ever.

Not even Carol had him this tied into knots.

The memory of his wife walking out on him, the devastation she left behind and the pity he'd seen in her eyes when he asked—hell, begged—her to give their marriage a second chance hit him in the gut like a kick from one of Jarrett Deeks's horses. And the thought of seeing that same pity in Darcy's eyes…

"I can't do this."

She took half a step back, her face paling, as she crossed her arms over her chest as if trying to ward off a chill…or maybe to block out the cold bite of his words. Still, though, she didn't look away as she asked, "Can't do what?"

She was going to make him say it, and he owed her, if not the whole truth, then at least an explanation. But everything he thought to say sounded like lame excuses even in his own head. Finally, he blurted out, "Most days, I can barely figure out how to be a single dad. I don't know how to do that and try to handle any kind of relationship."

"Funny, you seemed to be *handling* it just fine a half hour ago." Fire sparked in her green eyes, but her anger wasn't enough to burn away the sheen of tears.

Another emotion slammed into his chest at the sight. "Darcy…I'm sorry. This never should have happened."

"Your idea of an apology still needs work. And your timing stinks. The next time you decide you can't handle a relationship, you might share that information before having sex."

Chapter Eight

"It's not fair!"

Standing one row over in the local drugstore, Darcy paused as she overheard the unmistakable sound of a female in distress. The complaint was one she could have echoed in that same almost-in-tears tone over the past several days.

She'd taken a chance, betting the attraction between her and Nick would somehow make him see they were meant to be together. But even though their lovemaking had been more amazing than she could have imagined, even though she'd surrendered wholeheartedly to her desire for Nick, what they'd shared hadn't breached the wall he'd built up around him. At least not beyond a few moments when he'd given into physical need.

And it really wasn't fair.

Darcy had been ready to take her frozen dinner and bottle of pain pills to the checkout when the young girl's protest from one aisle over had made her pause. The poor thing sounded so devastated, the weight of the world—or her world at least—filling her words. Darcy's heart went out to the girl only to boomerang back into her chest with a sudden thud when she heard a deep, familiar voice respond.

"You have a whole row to choose from, Maddie."

She had no trouble recognizing Nick's voice even if it had been nearly a week since she'd heard it—since the day he brought her home from his cabin and dropped her off with a muttered farewell.

Heat rose to her face, but the slow flush of memory at the wonder of making love to Nick was quickly burned away by the painful humiliation of his rejection. *Play with fire,* her conscience taunted, and Darcy swallowed, frozen in place despite a desperate urge to run.

On the other side of the aisle, the father-daughter argument continued. "You have to pick something, Maddie."

"They're all so boring."

"Well, everyone else will be boring, too, because this is all they have."

"Nuh-uh. Rachel has a folder with a unicorn on it and Bobby has one with a race car and—"

The little girl was still in the middle of her long list of friends with folders so much cooler than hers when Darcy finally started to move. Only she didn't head for the door but around the end cap to the other side of the aisle. She had seen Maddie from a distance before, but up close Darcy noticed the girl's resemblance to her gorgeous father. She had Nick's dark hair and warm skin tone, but bright blue eyes that swam with tears.

And Nick…as much as she tried to harden her heart, it went out to the poor guy. He looked frazzled, the basket in front of him loaded with books, tablets of paper, folders, and more pens, markers and pencils than she thought a kid could go through in a lifetime.

But judging by the tension in his stance, the frustration in his broad shoulders, he and his daughter were nowhere close to done with the list Maddie clenched in her hand.

With his back to her, Darcy could have left without him knowing she'd witnessed the familial struggle. Thoughts of the dark-eyed vet had taunted her all the more since the day at his cabin, and more than once, she'd catch herself reaching for her shoulder. Not with the old, ingrained fear from that long-ago dog bite, but with the much more recent memory of his lips brushing across the faded scars there.

They're scars, Darcy. Everyone has them whether you can see them or not.

He was right, of course, everyone had scars. Even Nick. But he protected his gaping wounds by keeping people at a distance. *Emotional distance,* she thought, her body heating at the memory of making love, when they'd been as physically close as people could be.

But the misery in the little girl's eyes called to her, and Clearville was a small town. She'd have to get used to seeing Nick around after having seen him naked. She'd been willing to take a chance, to risk her heart. That Nick wasn't willing to take that same chance was his problem, not hers. She wasn't going to slink around like a brokenhearted fool, not even if she was a brokenhearted fool.

She wasn't unaware that her timing for running into Nick couldn't have been worse. She was mentally and physically exhausted from working on her shop and she looked like hell, but no time like the present, right?

After wheeling her cart to within a few feet of theirs, she stepped around the basket. "Oh, excuse me." Squeezing past the two Pirellis, Darcy broke some of the tension by positioning herself between them as she studied the colorful binders Maddie had declared boring. She could feel both sets of eyes—watery blue and solid brown—as she pretended to debate over the selection of binders.

"Darcy."

Her name was a low growl, and hot chills raced down her spine as she remembered the last time he spoke her name like that. Against her lips, her jaw, her throat… Her body trembled at the memory even as she steeled herself to meet his gaze with a look of mock surprise. "Nick, hi. How are you guys doing?"

"We're fine." His slight stress on the first word told Darcy loud and clear to ignore whatever she'd overheard and to butt out, but if there was one thing she knew, it was how to make the customer happy.

"It's so hard to choose, isn't it?" she mused aloud. "I mean, green's my favorite color, but look how pretty this purple one is. And then this pink one will match the colors of my shop perfectly."

Digging the toe of her rainbow-colored tennis shoe into the store's linoleum floor, the little girl muttered, "They're just plain colors."

"That's what makes them so perfect. This way I can decorate them myself."

In the silence that followed, Darcy feared the daughter might be as hard to crack as the father, but eventually Maddie asked, "Decorate how?"

"Any way I want. Like I think the pink one would be perfect covered in red hearts. And the green one is the same color as the grass at the park, so I'd probably cover it with all different flowers. And the purple one… Well, everything goes with purple." Darcy nodded. "That settles it. Purple it is."

She tucked the purple folder beneath her arm and hid a smile when Maddie reached for a purple folder of her own. It was crazy to feel a rush of pleasure as if she'd passed some kind of test in winning over the little girl. Especially when her efforts weren't likely to win her any points with Nick....

"What kind of flowers and stuff?" Maddie asked.

"Well, you have everything you need already. You have glue and paper and markers. I bet you have stickers at home you could use or some pictures."

"I could use the pictures from my trip to San Francisco, huh, Dad?"

"Why don't you go take a look at the stickers?" Following her dad's suggestion, Maddie rushed to the end of the aisle, shoes squeaking on the floors, to check out what the store had to offer.

Leaving Darcy alone with Nick.

The bravado that had carried her this far disappeared without Maddie to act as a buffer, and the intimacy they'd shared came rushing back. The need, the hunger, the vulnerability that had left her heart wide open and led to her total surrender in his arms.

Too late, the desire to bolt kicked in.

"I should—"

"Wait." He caught her arm before she could turn away, the press of his fingers against her skin another reminder of his body sinking into hers. His dark gaze focused on her with enough scrutiny to make her squirm. But the uneasy buzz of nerves stilled, everything—her breath, her heartbeat—coming to a sudden stop as he reached up and touched her face.

"You look…tired."

Reality slammed back into her, erasing the fantasy of Nick stroking her cheek and telling her she looked beautiful. She ducked away and brushed the side of her face against her shoulder, embarrassment flooding her as she wondered what streak of grit or grime hard work had left behind. She hoped the quick rub of her cotton T-shirt had gotten rid of whatever it was. Unfortunately, it didn't do anything to erase the lingering feel of Nick's fingertips against her skin.

"You're being kind," she said with a quick laugh. "I look like crap."

"You look tired," he repeated, and Darcy wanted nothing more than to rest her head against his chest and feel the strength of his arms around her. "Is everything okay?"

The vulnerability of her need had her hiding behind a smile she didn't feel. "It's fine. I'm fine." His stare didn't waver in the slightest, and Darcy felt sorry for Maddie should she ever try to get away with anything while under her dad's watchful eye. "I just had a bit of a run-in with my landlord."

The teasing comments she'd made didn't seem so funny now that Darcy had a good idea why the spot kept losing renters. "I thought I had everything worked out in the contract, but then Mrs. Leary stopped by and—"

"The Learys are your landlords?" Nick asked with a frown, and Darcy immediately realized her mistake.

From what she'd heard, the Learys, like Nick's family, had lived in Clearville for generations, and she wondered how badly she'd stuck her foot in her mouth. "You'd think I'd have learned by now. Small town, right? You know them. Of course you know them. Your families go back for decades, and you've all been friends for years—"

His sudden snort cut off her words. "I know I haven't made the best impression on you, but at least give the rest of my family some credit. We have a history with the Learys, but it's not a friendly one."

It took a moment for the rest of his words to sink in. Darcy had gotten caught on the phrase *I haven't made the best impression on you* and the hint of regret she'd heard in his tone.

"So what did Marlene want?"

"I'm not sure," she told Nick. "When I first looked into renting the spot, I met with Mr. Leary who, honestly, didn't seem to care what I did with the space as long as I paid my rent on time. But then—"

"You met Marlene."

Darcy nodded. She'd been almost finished working for the day, having torn up the existing scuffed and dented baseboards, pulled out dozens of nails left behind as souvenirs from previous shopkeepers and patched and prepped the walls for paint. She'd felt as limp and wilted as the damp bandanna she'd been using to hold back her hair from her face when Marlene Leary had unexpectedly dropped by.

Darcy had explained how the details of the remodeling were all written into the contract she'd signed, but that hadn't been good enough. So she told the woman about the changes she had planned.

About the fresh color scheme—a contrast between soft, sweet pink and strong, sophisticated black. About the tables at the front of the store, loaded with testers for customers to try as soon as they stepped inside. About the front window display she wanted to decorate like a romantic, old-fashioned dressing room rather than the cold, clinical feel of a department store beauty counter. And about the vintage crystal chandelier she'd found at The Hope Chest…

Caught up in her own excitement, Darcy had slowly realized Marlene Leary wasn't embracing her vision. If anything, the woman's frown had darkened. "Vintage," she sniffed. "I'll never understand how Hope Daniels has stayed in business selling other people's unwanted castoffs."

Unwanted castoffs…

If she hadn't been so tired, Darcy was sure the woman's comment would have bounced harmlessly aside. After all, her mother had raised her to be tougher than that. But Alanna was gone, and after days of feeling that loss so keenly, Marlene Leary's words had struck a painful blow at Darcy's greatest vulnerability.

Unwanted—that was how she'd always felt knowing her father had walked away before she was born. And Aaron had cast her off quickly enough when he feared the truth surrounding her birth might become a liability to his political career.

And then there was Nick…

"You should have called me," he said.

"What?"

"If you needed help, you should have called me."

Too startled by his comment, she couldn't help blurting out, "Why would I call you, Nick?"

He flinched as if struck by her words, but nothing in the way they had left things made her think he wanted to hear from her. "Darcy, I—"

"Don't." Cutting off what she was sure was an apology, she whispered, "You don't have to feel guilty, Nick. We both knew what we were doing."

Shivers streaked up her arm as he stroked his thumb against her flesh, making her question the truth in her words even before he cryptically asked, "Did we?"

Fortunately, Maddie broke the moment as she raced over, stumbling over her colorful shoes and scattering the packets of stickers across the scuffed linoleum. Her face turned bright red as she dropped to her knees and scrambled to pick up the stickers.

Eager to focus on something other than Nick, Darcy eased away from his touch, a little surprised he hadn't pulled away from her the moment Maddie turned back toward them. As she bent down to help, memories of her own childhood as the shy, awkward new girl who never really fit in came to mind, and Darcy's heart went out to Nick's daughter.

"You know," she said in a quiet murmur, "I drop stuff all the time."

"Really?"

"Really," she confided with a wink that brought a smile to the girl's face.

"Will these— Do you think these stickers will work?"

Glancing through the plastic packages at a mix of all things girlie, she said, "I think those will be perfect. You'll have a folder that will be just for you, decorated with all your favorite things."

Maddie beamed as she dropped the stickers and folder into the basket, and Nick asked, "Now can we finish with the rest of this list? I'd like to have this shopping done by the time you're ready to graduate."

"Dad—" his daughter sighed with an exaggerated rolling of her eyes "—I'm only eight!"

"So I keep telling myself," he said wryly. "Now, thank Ms. Dawson for her help and let her get back to her shopping."

"Thanks, Ms.— Hey." Maddie's eyes lit as she glanced between Darcy and her father. "Are you the lady with the puppies?"

Darcy managed a laugh, still somewhat amazed that she had a houseful of dogs, never mind that it was something she was evidently known for. She wouldn't go so far as to say she'd conquered her fear, but she'd made some pretty big strides, especially with the puppies. They were so cute and clumsy she couldn't help letting down her guard. Just starting to take their first stumbling steps, they frequently fell on their faces or tumbled over one another.

She'd read online about using a small plastic kiddie pool to keep the puppies contained and to help with cleaning up after them, but she had a feeling it wouldn't be long before Bo—the smallest yet most adventurous of the four—made a break for the outside world.

"I'm the lady with the puppies, but you can call me Darcy."

"My dad told me all about the puppies."

"Did he?" Darcy murmured, glancing at Nick, who responded with an almost guilty shrug. It was a sure bet the little girl wanted a puppy—something Nick might have mentioned to Darcy since she had four of them in need of good homes.

"They're so cute when they're little, but they'll be bigger before you know it," the little girl said with a wise-beyond-her-years awareness. "Then you'll have all kinds of things to teach them. Like how to fetch and roll over and shake. Oh, and how to walk on a leash 'cause you have to show 'em how. They don't just know how to do that on their own." She wrinkled her nose. "You have to clean up after them, too. That's not the fun part." Maddie sighed. "Puppies are a big responsibility."

It didn't take a genius to figure out where Maddie had heard that phrase. Leave it to Nick to point out the responsibility. Still, Darcy found something so endearing about seeing his strong, serious features reflected in such a dainty, feminine girl even though she hoped *that* wasn't the only reason why she felt such a pull toward the little girl.

No, it was more than simply seeing Nick in his daughter. Maddie was definitely her own person with her own ideas as she proved by asking her father, "Can we go see the puppies? Please, please, please."

As Nick gazed down at his daughter's adorable, up-turned face, Darcy's breath caught in her chest as she waited for his response. Self-preservation urged her to step in, to put an end to the possibility of spending any more time with Nick. But her foolish heart echoed Maddie's words. *Please, please, please.*

But Nick was made of stronger stuff, and he shook his head. "Not tonight. We're having a family dinner at my parents," he said by way of explanation as he met Darcy's gaze over his daughter's head. "We try to get together once a week. Sometimes it's only a few of us. Other times we have a houseful."

"Sounds fun," Darcy replied with what she figured was a weak smile. Theirs had never been a large family, but she and her mother had spent plenty of time seated at their small table, sharing stories about how their days had gone. She could have used one of those family dinners right about now. How she would love to have someone to pour out her heart to about her conflicted feelings for the man in front of her!

"*Loud* is how it usually sounds," Nick corrected. "Lots of arguing but lots of laughter, too." He shifted his feet as if weighing a decision, the shopping cart squeaking as its wheels inched forward and back again. "We, um, need to get going. We have to pick up dessert on the way."

"From Aunt Debbie's bakery?" Maddie asked, her disappointment over the puppies assuaged by the promise of dessert.

"Yeah, from Debbie's."

Nick's gaze sliced toward Darcy and then cut away, but the quick glance was enough to make her wonder. Did Nick have something going on with the pretty blonde baker? Yet how did that fit in with his speech about how Maddie was his first priority and he didn't have time to start any kind of relationship?

"She's not really my aunt like Aunt Sophia is," Maddie explained, "but she said I could call her that."

"That's…nice."

And it was. It spoke to the close relationship Debbie Mattson had with the Pirellis…and Nick.

Swallowing hard, Darcy forced a smile. "Well, I'll let you go then. Maddie, it was nice meeting you. Enjoy your dinner."

"You, too," he said automatically, and Darcy did her best to hold her head high and ignore the way his gaze dropped to the somewhat pathetic, single-serving frozen dinner sitting in her basket as she wheeled her cart away.

Chapter Nine

It didn't take a genius to realize he'd blown it with Darcy big-time.

For one afternoon, she'd made Nick forget his responsibilities, his doubts, his insecurities as a divorced, single father. With her in his arms, he'd simply been a man making love to a sassy, sexy, sensual woman who made him feel more awake and alive than he had in years.

And then the camp counselor had called, and all those responsibilities, doubts and insecurities came crashing back down. He'd rushed Darcy out of the house as if she were someone to be ashamed of. She'd given him those golden, glorious hours in her arms, and he'd tarnished them in minutes.

And he'd hurt her doing it.

He wasn't a player like Travis Parker, out to get what he could from a woman before casting her aside. His parents had raised him to respect women and to look out for them, a protective streak that had grown even stronger once he became a father to a little girl.

Which brought him back to Maddie and the newest dilemma that kept him from driving straight to Darcy's house and offering her the apology she deserved.

After one meeting, his daughter seemed as taken with Darcy as he was.

When can we go to Darcy's house to see the puppies?

What did Darcy name the puppies again?

Do you think Darcy would let me teach the puppies to fetch?

Maddie's obsession with the dogs he'd anticipated. Her fascination with Darcy was something that caught him completely off guard. He should have seen this coming. Wasn't Maddie's rush toward her preteen years and her need for a female presence the reason Nick had finally taken stock of his own life and admitted his own longing for someone to share his life with?

"Do you think Darcy will like my folder?"

Nick glanced over at the passenger seat. His daughter was bent over the purple folder they'd purchased earlier that day, still planning out the perfect placement for each and every sticker.

"It's your folder, Maddie. All that matters is whether or not you like it."

Slanting him a glance from the corner of her eye, she sighed, his answer clearly not the right one.

"You know, your aunt Sophia is back from her trip, so you can show her your folder tonight," he said, hoping to appease his daughter's need for a woman's presence. "And your grandmother will want to see it, too."

Maddie sighed again, but after a moment's pause asked, "What's for dinner tonight?"

"Lasagna."

"Yum, Grandma's lasagna is the best."

That was one thing he and his daughter could definitely agree on. He could practically taste the layer upon layer of hearty pasta and melted, stretching cheese. The scent of made-from-scratch sauce—tomato, oregano, onion, garlic—would fill the whole house, and the food would be second only to the love and laughter filling the Pirelli table.

His mouth was already watering when his thoughts flashed back to the lone and lonely frozen container of cardboard pasta in Darcy's basket.

He should have invited her.

The offer had been on the tip of his tongue while they'd stood together in the back-to-school aisle. The crazy thought arrowed through his head again, striking with a certainty that defied all logic, all reason, all sense of self-preservation. And yet the image of Darcy, alone, eating nothing more than a few squares of tasteless ravioli from a plastic tray had grabbed hold and refused to let go.

Not that he blamed her for wanting something quick and easy. He'd seen for himself how tired she was. Her hair had been caught back with a dark blue bandanna, revealing a face wiped free of makeup. Even without artifice, her skin had been flawless, making the dark circles beneath her eyes more apparent.

But she still looked more beautiful than any woman he'd ever known.

She had good reason to be exhausted, he thought as he slowed to drive by her shop. Even from outside the building and with only the faint security lighting from inside, he could see parts of what she'd accomplished so far. Spackle polka-dotted the walls and new lengths of baseboard and half-sheet paneling leaned against the front counter, waiting for installation. He wondered if Darcy planned to handle those jobs, too, if she really thought she could do it all.

Why would I call you?

Her question hit him like a sucker punch even though he damned well deserved it. But he was the oldest, the responsible one. A guy people looked up to and did call when they needed a hand, not just in his own family but in Clearville, too. Knowing Darcy wouldn't ask him for help because of the way he'd treated her left a sick feeling in his stomach.

He'd done his share of remodeling and knew how dirty, sweaty and just plain *hard* that kind of work was. Carol, for all her love of redecorating, didn't believe her part in the process should involve anything more than flipping through a magazine, clicking a mouse or writing a check. The thought of doing any of it herself would never have crossed her mind.

His mother had taught him long ago not to judge a book by its cover, but Nick couldn't help wondering if he'd done Darcy a greater disservice. Was he not only judging her by her looks, but judging her by his ex-wife? Two city girls, cut from the same designer cloth?

The similarities were there; Nick couldn't deny that. But there were differences, too. Darcy's bravery in facing her fears. Her determination to make her mother's dream come true. Her longing to find some connection with her past. Her easy laughter and the way it reached out and shook something loose inside him....

Pulling up to a stop in front of Bonnie's Bakery, he told his daughter, "I'm going to run in and pick up the cake. Do you want to come in?"

"Can I stay here? I'm almost done." Maddie held up the folder, which he had to admit had been a great idea. The once boring notebook was now a colorful collage of all things Maddie.

And Darcy would love it.

Holding back a sigh of his own, he said, "I'll be right back. Stay in the car."

Normally, the safety reminder would have drawn another eye roll and an I-know-Dad response, but instead, Maddie simply nodded. She studied her project, a frown of concentration pulling at her brows as she debated over her few remaining stickers.

So serious…

No one needed to tell Nick where his daughter got that tendency from. It was passed down from his DNA as obviously as his dark hair and olive skin had been. But Nick didn't want his daughter to take after him. He wanted her to have fun, to be a kid, but if teaching by example was the best way to go, he didn't even know where to start. It had been so long since he'd relaxed; some days he wondered if he still knew how.

Shaking off the thought, he climbed from the car and walked toward the bakery. He expected to see Debbie behind the counter, but instead one of the teenagers from the high school was manning the register.

"Hey, Doc," the young girl greeted him as the ring of the bell over the door faded away. "Debbie said you'd be coming by." She slid a white cake box across the glass counter, and he could plainly see his name written in black wax pencil across the top along with the words *piña colada*.

"I ordered her chocolate fudge cake," he pointed out. He always bought chocolate cake.

The teen grinned. "Debbie said you liked this one better."

How could he argue that point? The coconut-pineapple combination was the best cake he'd tasted in, well, ever. It was all the things he had said it was—unusual, different, exotic. But that wasn't what he wanted…was it?

The cashier's smile started to fade when Nick didn't

respond, and she tentatively added, "She said it's on the house…or I can box up another cake if you'd like."

All he had to do was ask, and he could take the same cake he always brought to dinner. Chocolate fudge meant no questions would be asked, no explanations needed to be given. He'd be doing what was expected, same as always, nothing unusual.

Maybe it was only dessert, but he couldn't expect things to change if he kept following the same path and making the same decisions he always made, could he?

His heartbeat kicked into overdrive as he tucked the box under his arm and hurried back to the SUV.

Maybe it was time for something out of the ordinary.

One of the benefits of having a houseful of beauty products was indulging in them, Darcy thought during her long, hot soak in a tub filled with lavender-scented bath salts. Closing her eyes and breathing deeply, she allowed the warm water to soothe the ache in her muscles and the one in her heart.

Later, determined to let her worries drain away with the water from her bath, she slipped into a pair of silk pajamas, even though it was still early, and twisted her hair into a messy bun. As she smoothed on the tropical-scented moisturizer she always wore, she felt better than she had in days.

Her TV dinner awaited her, but she bypassed the freezer on her way to the laundry room. She filled the dog bowl with kibble and set it a few feet away from the kiddie pool. The mama dog warily stepped out, keeping one eye on Darcy while gulping down the meal. The few seconds barely gave her enough time to place fresh towels in the makeshift puppy kennel. The three-foot distance was part of the truce between them, but Darcy had formed a habit of talking to the dog, mimicking Nick's low murmur.

"From what I've read, these guys can start eating a little food soon. Bet that will make things easier on you."

Not that it would be easy on Darcy, seeing as she needed to talk to Nick about the best way to introduce the puppies to something other than their mother's milk.

So far, she hadn't found anything that could wipe Nick from her mind. Physical challenges certainly hadn't been enough. Each time she heard footsteps outside her shop, her heart would skip a beat.

Which was ridiculous since he'd said and done nothing to make her think he would come by. In fact, hadn't just about every conversation they'd had ended with one or both of them agreeing they didn't want any kind of relationship? Sex didn't change that. Not even really amazing sex.

With her focus on the mama dog, an unexpected knock at the door made her jump. Walking into the living room, she ran her hands down her thighs. She hadn't anticipated company when she'd pulled on the matched set of silk pajamas—a pale blue camisole, shorts and knee-length robe.

She was still debating over answering the door or asking her visitor to wait on the porch while she went to change when the knock came again, followed by a quiet voice. "Darcy? It's Nick."

Indecision gone, she hurried to the front door and pulled it open. The summer sun had yet to set, the final rays peeking through the trees and casting a warm glow on the side of his face. He'd changed from the clothes he had on earlier—the button-down shirt and slacks that comprised his office wardrobe—to a soft gray T-shirt and well-worn jeans.

"Nick, what are you doing here? Is everything okay?" The words were out before she could stop them, and she felt a rush of heat flood her face. As if *she* would be the one the strong, self-assured vet would come to in an emergency!

"Yeah, everything's fine." Despite the reassurance, the shift of his weight on the balls of his feet made Darcy think he might bolt at any minute.

"Would you like to come in?" She opened the door a bit wider, and he glanced over her shoulder inside and then back out to the SUV at the end of her drive.

"I can't. Maddie's in the car waiting." Running his hand through his hair to grasp the back of his neck, he seemed to come to some kind of decision. "See, the thing is, my family's Italian. Right now, my mother is likely pulling out a lasagna pan roughly the size of your kitchen table from the oven. It's enough food to feed my whole family with leftovers to share, and she would slap me upside the head if she knew I let you eat that frozen cardboard pasta instead of inviting you."

"I'm not sure I like the idea of you 'letting' me eat anything." It was all a little too Marie Antoinette, which had Darcy thinking of cake. And of Debbie Mattson, the pretty blonde baker, who'd made Nick's dessert for the evening. Who may or may not have something going on with the handsome vet.

"You know what I mean. So have you already eaten?"

"Not yet." She tried to eat healthy most nights, but she'd been too tired lately to bother making an entire meal just for herself. Somehow, the single-serving frozen meals didn't emphasize that she'd be eating alone nearly as much as dishing up one plate from a recipe meant for four.

"Then come with me."

"To your family dinner?" She didn't think anything could have surprised her more, but shock wasn't enough to keep her questions at bay. "What are you doing, Nick?"

A corner of his mouth kicked up in a crooked grin that did ridiculous things to her heartbeat as he admitted, "Something I damn sure didn't plan, I can tell you that much."

"The last time we did something unplanned, you ended up regretting it, and I don't want to be the reason—"

"I don't regret it. Not one second of it." The half smile was gone, replaced by the seriousness more in keeping with the man she knew. "Only the way I acted afterward," he added.

"We made a mistake."

"I made the mistake by not telling you how…incredible it was between us. So incredible that for a while nothing else mattered except the two of us." He stopped for a moment, his gaze searching her face as if trying to judge her willingness to listen to what he had to say, her willingness to trust him. "But you have to understand that, for the last five years, the only 'two of us' in my life has been me and my daughter."

It was his love for his daughter that did it every time, Darcy thought with a sigh. How could she stay angry with him for putting Maddie first?

"I get that, Nick, I do." And she appreciated it more than he could probably understand. "You told me from the beginning you don't have room for anyone else."

He winced a little at that. "I said a lot of things, but what I'm asking for now is a chance to start over. To welcome you to town instead of trying to push you away." Reaching up, he brushed back a loose strand of hair from her cheek. "You've had a rough week, and sometimes there's no better cure than a home-cooked meal."

The caring in his gaze washed over her with the same warmth as her earlier bath, leaving her skin feeling flushed and damp. And crazy or not, she said, "Okay, I'd like that."

He didn't actually smile, but the spark in his eyes made it clear he was glad she'd agreed.

"And Sophia will be there, so it's not like you'll be surrounded by strangers."

Nick's sister had been one of the first people Darcy had met when she moved to town. The petite brunette had stopped by within hours of Darcy signing the rental papers on the shop. So excited by how close she was to making her mother's dream come true, Darcy had spilled everything to the other woman—her hopes for The Beauty Mark, her need for a new start after her broken engagement. In return, Sophia had talked about her fiancé, Jake Cameron, their plans for their upcoming wedding and their own excitement over Sophia's pregnancy.

Since then, Sophia and Darcy had talked every few days, but with Sophia being out of town visiting her future in-laws for the past few weeks... Well, a lot had happened in that time. Not that Darcy would have shared everything with Nick's sister.

"I should also tell you that I may have told Maddie we could come back here and see the puppies after dinner if it's okay with you."

Remembering the little girl's excitement, Darcy nodded. "Of course she can. And now I better go change."

"It is just family, nothing fancy."

"I still think this might be a little too casual," she said, flicking the hem of her robe with her fingers.

"You wouldn't hear me complain," he murmured. "But then again, neither would my brothers, so yeah, you better go change."

"I'll be right back."

As Darcy backed from the room and hurried down the hall to her bedroom, she heard her front door shut and the sound of voices from outside the house. Maddie gave a delighted shout, and Darcy smiled as she searched through her tiny closet. The little girl was likely far more excited about seeing the puppies than she was about Darcy joining them for dinner, but that was okay. She felt excited enough—and nervous enough—for both of them.

Dinner with Nick's family.

Memories of her first meeting with Aaron's parents jabbed at her thoughts, threatening to break the bubble of Nick's invitation. The Utleys had been coldly polite during the formal dinner at the five-star restaurant Aaron had taken them to, and she should have realized then she could never live up to the expectations they had for their son's future wife. And that was before they found out she was the result of an illicit affair between her teenage mother and a prominent, powerful and *married* businessman.

Shoving aside those thoughts, she grabbed a wraparound dress with a blue-and-brown geometric print. Nick had said casual, but she wanted to make a good impression.

On Nick's family, her conscience goaded, *or on Nick?*

Because while there was nothing overly revealing about the dress, she'd always liked the way the crossover style hugged her waist and how the V-neckline arrowed between her breasts. Refusing to stop long enough to think about her choice, she added a chunky amber-colored necklace and matching bracelet and slid on a pair of strappy sandals.

Her hair, fortunately, was almost dry, so she wasted little time brushing it out before sweeping it back up in a large clip. Not wanting to leave Nick and Maddie waiting any longer than necessary, she dusted the bare minimum of powder and blush on her face. A single swipe of eyeliner on each lid, followed by a brush of mascara and dab of lip gloss, and she was ready to go.

Just as she was finishing, she heard the front door open again and called out, "I'm almost ready."

"No hurry. I called my folks to let them know we were running late...."

Nick's voice grew louder as she followed the sound down the hallway and into the kitchen, but the words came to an abrupt halt as she stepped into the room. She smiled, somehow not surprised Nick had sought out the stray dog—or maybe it was the other way around—and was kneeling on the floor, petting her.

He rose slowly, his gaze making the same gradual climb, starting at her sandals and working his way up. "You look…"

His voice trailed off again, and Darcy started having second thoughts. Her city-girl outfits stood out amid the casual cotton and denim wardrobes most of the town favored. "It's too much, isn't it? I—"

He caught her hand when she may well have backed out of the room and darted into her bedroom to change again. "You look amazing," he finished.

There was no mistaking the male appreciation written in his expression or her answering response as a small shiver raced down her spine. His gaze lowered to her lips, and she instinctively parted them on a breath of anticipation. Still holding her arm, Nick drew her closer and her pulse pounded as she waited for the heat of his mouth against hers…

The cold, wet touch at the back of her knee shocked a soft squeal out of her. Startled, she practically jumped into Nick's arms as she glanced over her shoulder at the dog who'd crouched almost flat to the floor at Darcy's sudden movement.

Nick's warm chuckle against her ear made Darcy realize she'd practically climbed him like a kitten up a tree in her need to escape. "Well, I wanted you back in my arms, but I can't say this is what I had in mind."

With fear giving way to embarrassment, she hid her face

in the crook of his shoulder and thought she just might stay there until he asked her to move. "I'm sorry."

She took another moment to memorize the feel of Nick's arms around her waist, his chest pressed to hers and their legs tangled together in a closer embrace than if they'd been slow dancing on a darkened, intimate dance floor. Finally, she took a cautious step away, keeping Nick between her and the dog still watching warily from a few feet away. "She startled me."

"I think that goes both ways." He knelt down again by the dog, reaching out a hand to let her sniff him before glancing back up at Darcy. "You haven't named her yet?"

"Not yet. With the puppies, it was easy. They didn't already have names. But you said she's around two, right? Somewhere along the way she had to have had a home, a name."

"I always thought a new name was fitting. New name, new start." He'd lowered his voice to a deep, mesmerizing murmur as his fingers disappeared into the dog's thick fur, and Darcy could see the tension start to flow away as the animal's two-tone eyes watched Nick with a look of complete trust.

"I'd like to keep her, but I don't know if it would be fair."

"What do you mean?"

"Well, look at her. She's ready to melt." Not that she blamed the dog. If Nick sank his hands into her hair and massaged her scalp, she'd be ready to sink down to the floor at his feet, too. "She deserves someone like you. Someone who isn't afraid."

"Here." Nick held out a hand. "You're perfectly safe."

Had anyone else urged her closer, Darcy's first instinct would have been to take a huge step backward. But his open palm and outstretched arm drew her toward him without even touching her, and when she was close enough for him to take her hand, she knew. She was safe.

As she sank down to her knees beside Nick, he quietly said, "See how still she is now? Like she's braced for something bad to happen?"

Looking closely, Darcy nodded. "Uh-huh."

"Well, that's all coming from you."

"Me? Why?"

"Can't you feel how tense you are? You arms? Your shoulders? I think you've left a permanent imprint on my hand."

Good thing she kept her nails short, or she might have drawn blood. Darcy forced her grip to relax. "Oh, my gosh. I am so sorry."

"I know you're afraid. But you've been carrying that fear around for years. Don't you think it's time to let go?"

She didn't know if she heard a hint of challenge in Nick's words, but there or not, she accepted it. She could do this. Reaching out a trembling hand, she touched the dog's back. She felt the flinch of muscle and her breath caught on a silent gasp.

Only...nothing happened. The dog didn't growl or snap or bite. She didn't even move as Darcy explored the short, smooth texture of her coat. After a few minutes, the dog turned her head and before Darcy had a chance to be afraid, took a quick, wet lick of her wrist. And Darcy laughed. A little shakily, maybe, but it was a laugh all the same.

Nick grinned at her. "We might make a dog lover out of you yet." He rose to his feet and pulled her with him.

Maybe it was the nerves still jumping through her stomach at taking the small step at conquering her fear or maybe it was the sight of that easy, relaxed smile on Nick's face, but Darcy was feeling somewhat invincible.

It was the only reason she could come up with for charging so boldly ahead.

"You know, it's funny."

"What?"

"Everything you just said about being afraid and letting go of the past… It's kind of what I've been wanting to say to you."

His recoil might not have been as obvious as hers, but Darcy could still sense that she'd caught him off guard. Rushing ahead before she lost her nerve, she said, "I've been afraid, too, you know. Coming here was about making a new start, but that also meant making some mistakes. Still, I'm willing to keep trying. Are you?"

"It's not so easy to forget about the past or to ignore the future when you have a child. I know I probably sound like a total hypocrite—"

"You sound like a father. Like a caring, loving father. I wouldn't expect anything less. And I'm not a single parent, but I know a thing or two about being raised by one."

"So did your mother manage to have it all? To raise a child and still have some kind of social life?"

"No. She just had me. She always joked that when she was in her golden oldies, she'd find her dream guy in a retirement home. A couple of gray-hairs madly in love."

Instead Alanna had died before more than a strand or two of gray touched her dark hair. Her mother's death had taught Darcy that she could plan all she wanted for tomorrow, but it was best to take advantage of today.

"I know Maddie will always be your first priority. All I'm asking is, do you think there could be room for something more? More than just being her dad?"

"Darcy—" The loud blast from the SUV's horn interrupted, and Nick closed his eyes but not before she saw a hint of relief in his dark gaze. "We should go."

Ignoring her own disappointment and the worry that his silence might be an answer in itself, she joked, "Saved by the horn."

She stopped to grab her purse off the couch in the living room and met Nick at the front door. He paused with his hand on the knob and turned to face her. "I want to say yes," he blurted out. "More than you can probably imagine. I want to say I can have more, *we* can have more, but it's hard to do when my daughter's leaning on the horn because I've made her wait five whole minutes."

The simmering frustration just beneath the surface went a long way to easing Darcy's disappointment. "It's okay, Nick."

"It's not," he argued, stubbornly resisting her efforts to let him off the hook. "You deserve better."

"For now, I think it's enough to know we both want more."

Chapter Ten

Stepping inside the Pirelli home, Darcy closed her eyes and took a deep breath. If the food tasted half as good as it smelled, dinner would be better than anything she'd had in the restaurants where Aaron liked to be seen. Already the atmosphere was an improvement over those trendy, overpriced places.

The front door opened from a wide, welcoming porch into a comfortable living room complete with floral couches and matching armchairs huddled around a rug spread over hardwood floors. Dozens of framed photographs lined a brick fireplace mantel and a large family portrait hung as a proud focal point above it.

This, she knew, was home.

Not the temporary fixer-uppers she and her mother had shared for a few months at a time before moving on, but a permanent, lasting home filled with history and memories and love. She wondered briefly if Nick knew how lucky he was to have such a solid, stable foundation, but a quick glance at his relaxed smile gave her an answer.

"Darcy!"

Sophia, Nick's sister, appeared in the doorway and rushed toward her as if it had been years rather than weeks since they'd seen each other. Her short mahogany hair was tucked behind her ears and, in a white sundress trimmed in eyelet lace, she looked as happy as a bride-to-be should. Darcy didn't know if it was a pregnancy glow or a "madly in love" glow, but her friend looked positively radiant. Her dark eyes glittered as she looked between Darcy and Nick. "I'm so glad you're here."

"Jeez, kid, guess you and I are chopped liver," Nick muttered to his daughter, who shot him a confused frown.

"Huh?"

"Of course I'm happy to see you, too." Sophia stretched on her tiptoes to kiss her eldest brother's cheek and then bent to hug her niece. "I'm just happy." She beamed.

Darcy glanced at Nick, who spun his finger in a circle at his temple with a pointed look at his sister. "Bridal fever," he mouthed silently.

Fighting laughter, she elbowed him in the ribs and asked Sophia, "Did you have a good trip?"

"I did! In fact, I can't wait to tell you all about it."

Latching on to Darcy's wrist, Nick's small but surprisingly strong sister started trawling her toward the living room doorway. "The guys are out back, Nick. We'll call you when dinner's ready."

Darcy glanced back at Nick helplessly, but he simply shrugged and left her to fend for herself. They were barely out of earshot in the dining room when the other woman whispered, "Oh, my gosh! You and Nick! I never would have imagined that. You and Sam, sure. Even Drew but—"

"Sophia, stop! Please," Darcy protested. "Nick and I

ran into each other at the store, and I think I offended your family's Italian heritage with my choice of frozen ravioli. Nick took pity on me and invited me to dinner."

"Oh, yeah," Sophia deadpanned. "Why else would he invite you to dinner? Pity, that's gotta be it." She crossed her arms over her expanding waistline and waited silently for Darcy to crack, but she held firm.

Finally Sophia lowered her arms. "Fine. But I really hope there's more to the story because I think you're exactly what Nick needs. Someone who can shake things up a bit, knock some of the rust off."

It was a tall order, especially since Darcy wasn't so sure Nick wanted all that shaking and knocking going on in his life.

"Somehow I doubt he'd agree with you on that."

"Don't be so sure. After Jake and I got engaged, Nick kind of hinted that he was ready to start dating again."

"He did?" Darcy asked in surprise. How did that fit in with Nick's "single father first" rule?

Sophia nodded. "Of course, I figured he'd try to find a woman from Clearville. Someone small town. Someone just like him, in other words."

"That's what Nick wants?"

A woman like Debbie Mattson? Darcy wondered, remembering Nick's odd reaction when his daughter mentioned the blonde baker's name.

"No. No!" Realizing how Darcy had taken her words, Sophia reached out and gave her arm an encouraging squeeze. "That's what he *thinks* he wants."

"I'm not sure I understand the difference." Not when everything Sophia thought Nick wanted was everything Darcy wasn't.

"He thinks he wants someone safe, someone who won't go to his head or make him risk his heart. But he'd never be happy with someone like that. Not head-over-heels happy the way he deserves to be."

Still mulling over Sophia's words, she followed the other woman into the kitchen.

"I don't think you've met my mom," Sophia said.

Vanessa Pirelli stood at the island, cutting French bread into thick slices. Her brown hair was styled in a sleek bob with a strand or two of gray showing through. Faint wrinkles fanned out from her green eyes when she smiled, the expression lighting her whole face. She was lovely in a natural, welcoming way, and just as her house had spoken so clearly of home, Vanessa was a woman who embraced the word *family.*

"Mrs. Pirelli, it's nice to meet you."

It was silly to be nervous, Darcy told herself as she reached for the older woman's hand. She had every reason to believe Mrs. Pirelli would be as gracious and welcoming as her daughter. But as Darcy met her gaze, she silently admitted how much she wanted Vanessa Pirelli to like her.

"Oh, please, call me Vanessa. I've been meaning to stop by and say hello and welcome you to town, but with Sophia's engagement and the wedding to plan—" She cut herself off, almost as if she had too much on her mind to complete a whole sentence.

"Believe me, I certainly understand that you've had your hands full," Darcy said, touched the woman would have even thought of reaching out to her at a time when her family had so much going on.

"From what I've heard, you've been pretty busy, too."

Darcy's good feeling evaporated like morning fog in the noonday sun. *You've been busy.* It sounded like an innocuous comment, but it was also the kind of vague, subtle remark her ex's mother had excelled at. Those cool, polite comments would leave Darcy's head spinning as she tried to figure out the meaning behind the words.

Aaron swore she was imagining things and that his mother was doing nothing more than making conversation. And Darcy had convinced herself Aaron was simply blind to his mother's faults. Far too late did she realize how clearly he saw things through his mother's eyes.

But Vanessa's gaze was straightforward and direct as she added, "I've heard about the remodeling going on at the space you've rented, and from what our local mailman tells me, you have so many packages arriving each day, he feels like he's in the middle of the Christmas rush."

Darcy's immediate sense of relief was followed by an equally powerful feeling of shame. What was she thinking to compare Vanessa Pirelli to Barbara Utley? The two women couldn't have been any less alike!

"I have been busy at the shop, but I really want to become a part of this town. Thank you for having me over tonight."

"You're welcome, and I'm sure you're going to fit in just fine. But remember, we take things a little slower around here. Give it some time." Vanessa glanced over at her daughter, who'd circled the island to slather garlic-infused butter over the pieces of bread she'd already sliced. "Sophia and I were talking earlier, and I realized that I knew your mother."

"You did?" In an evening of surprises, this was yet another she hadn't seen coming. As Vanessa said, time did go by more slowly in small towns, but it had been nearly thirty years since her mother had lived in Clearville, and somehow Darcy hadn't expected anyone to still remember Alanna. Sometimes it felt as if she was the only one to remember her mother at all.

"I used to babysit her when I was a teenager and she

was a little girl. I can see a lot of her in you." Circling the island, Vanessa took Darcy's hands. Compassion brimmed in her eyes. "Sophia told me that she passed away recently. I am so sorry."

The unexpected touch and heartfelt sympathy brought the ache of tears to her throat. Losing her mother had been hard. So, too, was the fact that Darcy had so few people to share in her grief. In many ways, she and her mother were alike. With all the moving they'd done together, neither of them had searched outside their tight-knit mother-daughter unit for close friendships.

They'd always had acquaintances, but those casual relationships had fallen away during the long months when Alanna was struggling to recover from the accident and Darcy was spending as much time as she could by her mother's side. How different life would have been if she and her mother had moved back to Clearville sooner!

"Thank you," she said huskily. "I miss her every day."

"You might not have been born here, but this is where you're from. So let me be the first to welcome you home, Darcy Dawson."

As Maddie ran over toward the swings where her grandfather had promised to push her "super high," Nick joined his brothers and future brother-in-law at a weathered picnic table that had seen its share of family gatherings. His brother Drew and Jake Cameron sat on benches facing each other, while Sam leaned against the table, one foot braced on a cooler.

The three of them fell silent as he approached, but Nick doubted he'd be lucky enough for the reprieve to last. Sam kicked open the cooler and reached inside for a beer that he tossed to Nick.

"Damn, Nick. Ten years hasn't slowed you down at all, has it? You still move fast."

Nick frowned at his youngest brother. "What are you talking about, Sam?"

"Darcy! You've been seeing her how long and you're already bringing her home to meet the parents?"

Meet the parents...

"No. It's not— No! It's just dinner."

"Yeah, right. Just dinner." Sam tipped his beer in Jake's direction. "You were here how long before you and Sophia got engaged?"

"Couple of weeks," he responded with a slightly apologetic shrug at Nick.

"See?" Sam said. "Your days are numbered."

As much as Nick loved both of his brothers, from the time Sam had been born, he'd had the uncanny knack of getting under Nick's skin. Even knowing his little brother purposely set out to annoy him didn't keep him from being any less annoyed. "It's one dinner," he pointed out.

"Uh-huh. And how many family dinners did you and Carol have before you told everyone the two of you were getting married?" Sam challenged, his smug smile revealing he knew the answer as well as Nick did. By the time Nick brought Carol to meet his family, they were already engaged. Their announcement to his family after dessert had been only a formality.

"That's not the same thing," he argued. "Carol and I had been dating for a few months before I brought her home."

With Carol in San Francisco and Nick in Clearville, seeing each other hadn't been easy. He often thought the logistics of him spending weekends with her at her apartment or both of them traveling to meet at some midpoint location would have soon ended their long-distance relationship. But before their desire for each other had a chance to flicker out, the hotel where Carol worked had been bought by another company. Staying on would have meant a transfer to New Orleans and a sudden, unexpected end to their affair.

Not wanting to lose her, he'd proposed. Not wanting to move to New Orleans, she'd accepted.

Taking a swig of beer, Nick tried to wash away some of the bitterness. He didn't think that was the only reason Carol had married him, but the loss of her job had certainly been part of it. Later on, she'd regretted giving up her career, blaming him even for being stuck in Clearville when she could have been letting the good times roll in Louisiana.

He'd hoped his dream of making a home and raising a family in Clearville would become Carol's dream, too, but it didn't work that way. *Nontransferable,* he thought, like some kind of fine print he hadn't seen until it was too late.

And yet wasn't that exactly what Darcy was trying to do? To live out her mother's dream? He couldn't help wondering if once she opened her mother's shop, she'd then be ready to move on. To her own dreams…whatever they might be.

And yet, she was working hard, remodeling the store. She'd put in far more effort in a short period of time than Carol had put into anything in the four years she'd lived in Clearville.

An image of Darcy's pale face in the drugstore that afternoon flashed through his mind. She'd looked ready to drop. He hadn't seen any signs of that exhaustion this evening, but if she kept at it, she'd wear herself out long before her grand opening.

He didn't want that to happen.

He didn't know if fulfilling her mother's dream would mean the end to Darcy's time in Clearville or if it would only be the beginning, but either way, he wanted her to enjoy that success. He couldn't control what happened after, but the work that still needed to be done now, he could have a hand in.

Aware he was completely changing the subject, Nick looked over at Drew. "I know you've been busy lately," he said, referring to the trips his brother had been making back and forth between their hometown and Seattle. As a custom home builder, Drew was used to demanding clients, but this reclusive millionaire wanted face-to-face meetings without rearranging his schedule to travel to Clearville. "But do you know of anyone who might be available to give Darcy a hand with the remodeling over the next few days? And don't say Travis Parker."

Nick didn't care if they'd had only a few meaningless dates; he didn't like the idea of that man being anywhere near Darcy. Hell, he didn't really like the idea of any man spending time with her. Any man other than him.

Drew gave a scoffing laugh. "You know me better than that. I wouldn't recommend Parker for remodeling a bird-house." He tipped back his beer, but Nick recognized the stall tactic. His brother had a ton of them. Drew had always been the type to think before he spoke, to examine a situation from all angles, analyze structural strengths and weaknesses.

And he couldn't help wondering how much he'd given away with his request.

Sam might be like a persistent mosquito, always buzzing and biting along the surface, but Drew would dig deeper, going to the heart of the matter. And right now, Nick didn't want anyone examining his feelings for Darcy too closely.

Including himself.

Setting the beer can on the table, Drew finally said, "I think I know just the guy for the job."

His brother's easy answer caught Nick off guard. He'd

hoped Drew might agree but— "Who is it? And are you sure he's free on such short notice?"

"It's me, and yeah, I'm free. My trip to Washington's been postponed a few days. I already have my crews set, since I thought I'd be gone, so unless an emergency comes up, I've got time. How about you, Sam?"

Thanks to their dad, all of the Pirelli sons knew a thing or two about construction and about cars, but it was Drew and Sam who'd turned those hobbies into professions. Anytime one of them needed a hand, the others were quick to join in.

"Will's been begging me to give him more responsibility, so I'm sure I can free up a couple hours tomorrow, and then the shop's closed on Sunday. Between the three of us, I bet we can knock it out in two days. What about you, Jake? Willing to make it four?"

Jake's smile was a little wry as if he already anticipated what was coming, but the future Pirelli in-law said, "I'll run it by Sophia to make sure we don't have any pre-wedding plans, but I'm sure she'll be glad we're all helping Darcy out."

"Run it by Sophia," Sam echoed beneath his breath but loud enough for all to hear. "See, Nick? You see what's ahead of you? It's sad, man, I'm telling you."

Ignoring him, Nick said, "Thanks, guys, I appreciate this, and I know Darcy will, too."

Or she would as soon as he convinced her to let them help.

Leaving the beer he'd barely touched on the picnic table, he turned to head back to the house. In the fading sunlight, his youngest brother's voice carried across the grassy yard. "Oh, no, he's not dead man walking at all."

"Shut up, Sam."

* * *

Welcome home...

Two simple words, but Darcy hadn't felt the warm embrace of home since her mother's accident. Maybe not even before that. Although Alanna had tried to make each place feel like home, they'd both known how temporary their stay would be.

Embarrassed by the rush of emotion at Vanessa's warm welcome, Darcy had asked to use the powder room before Vanessa or Sophia could see the tears in her eyes. But instead of heading back to the kitchen afterward, she slipped out the front door to the porch swing she'd noticed when Nick had first pulled up to the house.

Over the faint squeak of the chains, Darcy could hear the sound of male laughter and Maddie's happy squeals from the backyard. The sounds were unfamiliar, and yet they felt so right. The setting sun cast the pines surrounding the house into silhouette and shadow, but even in the growing darkness, she recognized Nick's broad-shouldered form as he circled the side of the house.

The boards creaked beneath his boots as he climbed the steps and crossed the porch, and Darcy stilled the swaying swing in invitation. "What are you doing out here by yourself?" he asked as he sat beside her. The seat rocked as he angled toward her and stilled. He brushed his thumb across her cheekbone. "What's wrong?"

She ducked her head and wiped her eyes. "Your sister and mother have been so nice."

"And that made you cry?"

"It was just...unexpected."

"You didn't expect my family to be nice?"

Darcy heard the frown in his voice and shook her head. She was making a mess of her explanation, but how could she expect Nick to understand unless she told him about Aaron?

"The last family dinner I was invited to ended in a broken engagement," she blurted out. "Mine."

Darcy sensed his shock—whether at the way her engagement had ended or that she'd been engaged in the first place, she didn't know. But all he asked was, "What happened?"

"I'm not sure what kind of woman Aaron's parents thought he'd marry, but it certainly wasn't me. I told myself what they thought didn't matter. Turned out it mattered to Aaron a lot."

Sitting beside Nick now, though, she had a hard time remembering the sound of her fiancé's voice, the exact color of his eyes, the differing shades in his blond hair. Aaron's image was like a faded photograph compared to Nick in full, rich dimension.

Nick swore beneath his breath, his voice incredulous as he demanded, "He broke up with you because his parents told him to?"

There was more to it than that, but nothing Darcy felt like getting into right then. Staring out into the shadows shifting across the yard, she simply stated, "Actually, I'm the one who broke it off."

She could feel his gaze on the side of her face before he reached up and drew a finger along her jaw, turning her toward him. "The guy was a jerk."

"So what about you?"

"Me? Okay, yeah, I admit I've been something of a jerk, too—"

"No," Darcy protested with a laugh before sobering. "What about you and Maddie's mother?"

"Carol," he answered. "All I ever wanted was to live here

in Clearville. To get married, raise a family and do the job I love. I fooled myself into thinking she wanted that, too."

"What did she want?"

"More," he said simply. "More than Clearville, more than me, more than Maddie. Unfortunately, I refused to see that until the day I came home and found that she'd left."

Feeling Nick had more to say, Darcy waited. A long silence followed, finally broken by a high-pitched giggle and robust laughter drifting over from the swings where Maddie and her grandfather were playing. The sound made Nick smile, and he said, "When Carol first left, my parents were amazing. They stepped in right away, my mother, especially. I was struggling, trying to do everything on my own, and after raising four kids, my mom knows more about being a parent than I can hope to learn. I never had a doubt that Maddie was better off with my mom than she'd been with Carol. But after a while, I started to wonder if she'd be better off without me, too."

"Oh, Nick."

"I wouldn't have abandoned her. I never considered that. Not once." Fierce determination glowed in his dark eyes, visible even in the fading daylight. "But I did think of how easy it would be to let my parents do a little more here, a little more there. But deep down I knew those 'little bits' were pieces of our lives—mine and Maddie's. And if I gave them away, I'd never get them back."

"Does Carol ever come see Maddie?"

"Come here? No, but Maddie visits her in San Francisco."

Remembering the watchful eye Nick had kept on his daughter even on Clearville's friendly streets, Darcy said, "That must be tough."

"I hate it. I hate shared custody. Not being at Maddie's side, thinking that something might happen to her and I'd be hundreds of miles away and helpless to do anything about it—"

He cut himself off, but only after telling Darcy more than she expected, opening up about his love for his daughter and his vulnerability where she was concerned.

He exhaled a deep breath before asking, "So tonight… Was it too much?"

"Too much?"

"Sam's been giving me a hard time for bringing you to meet my family on a first date."

"Is this a date?" And did *first* imply that there would be a second?

He gave a rough laugh. "Hell, it's been so long since I've been on one, I was hoping you'd tell me. If you don't know either, we might both be in trouble."

The swing rocked as Nick leaned closer, upsetting the tenuous balance that had kept them still. Though the chains swayed in a gentle, easy motion, she felt as though she were soaring through the air when he pulled her close. The final lingering rays of sunset had disappeared, but his touch heated her skin with all the promise of a brand-new day.

The kiss was everything a first kiss should have been— everything they'd denied themselves by giving into the rush of passion instead of slowing down to enjoy these initial, innocent steps. The simple, sweet hello of his mouth against hers. The unhurried, getting-to-know-you parting of lips. The tentative revealing of hopes and dreams and emotions as they opened up to each other. One kiss and Darcy knew.

She was definitely in trouble.

Chapter Eleven

"Now can we go see the puppies?" The long-suffering question came from Maddie as she climbed into the back-seat of the SUV.

Nick glanced over at Darcy as she buckled her seat belt. "It's up to you," he murmured, knowing she'd had a long day and giving her an easy out even though he didn't want the evening to end.

"We can't disappoint the puppies," she said, leaning around the seat to face his daughter. "I know they're so excited to meet you, Maddie."

"Yes!" She flashed a conspirator's wink back at Darcy, one Nick caught in the rearview mirror.

It wasn't the first shared moment Maddie and Darcy had during the evening.

Not long after their kiss on the porch, Vanessa called the family in to dinner, and by the end of the evening, Nick had decided Sam was right. He was crazy to have invited Darcy to a family dinner on their first date. Not because of any ideas her presence might create about their relationship, but because of all the ideas he had. Ideas he shouldn't be having with his parents and daughter sitting a few chairs away.

He'd felt as though his desire was written on his face for all to see, and he was endlessly grateful Sam had taken some kind of pity on him and hadn't called him out on it while passing the garlic bread.

Thoughts of their kiss played like a video on a loop, and he'd felt hypersensitive of every move she made—from wrapping her slender fingers around a fork to smoothing a napkin over her thighs to the small hum of appreciation she made at her first bite of lasagna. A sound almost identical to the one when they made love.

Trying to keep his focus off the woman at his side, he'd quickly noticed Maddie studying Darcy, mimicking her actions down to the napkin his daughter had placed in her own lap.

After all her questions that afternoon, he'd expected Maddie's fascination with Darcy's feminine touches. On the ride over to his parents', she'd asked about her dress, her shoes, her jewelry, her hair.

He tried to tell himself his daughter's obvious craving for a woman in her life wasn't a reflection on him. That each question didn't strike at the heart of his failure as a husband, as a father. That was what he told himself.

He just wasn't sure he believed it.

Once they reached Darcy's house, a sound he hadn't heard in far too long went a long way to easing his worries. Crouched down in the laundry room doorway, with her fingers tightly laced together beneath her chin as if doing all she could to keep from reaching out, Maddie giggled as one of the puppies took an awkward step before tumbling into its closest sibling.

Standing outside the doorway to the small room, Darcy murmured, "I'm surprised you and Maddie don't already have a dog." She kept her voice down as if not overhearing the words would keep Maddie from wanting to take all four puppies home with them.

Little chance of that, Nick knew. His daughter was clearly in love already. "I always had pets growing up. My poor mom learned early on that she might as well let me have a dog because if she didn't, I'd just as likely come home with an injured squirrel or rabbit or raccoon."

"Isn't that dangerous?"

"It can be. You never know how wild animals will react when cornered, especially if they are injured."

Darcy made a small sound, as if she was agreeing with what he was talking about and yet he wasn't talking about animals at all. Was that how she thought of him? Like an angry bear with his paw caught in a trap? He had to admit, he had felt caught between a rock and a hard place that day at his cabin. Trapped between his desires as a man and his duties as a father. And so he'd snapped.

Was that why he sensed Darcy keeping a distance between them? Because she'd learned her lesson and wouldn't risk another chance with him? Or was she simply doing what they'd agreed and taking things slow? It was hard to tell considering they hadn't been alone most of the evening. Other than the brief moment on the porch swing, they'd been surrounded by his family.

"So your mom let you have a dog," Darcy was saying, and Nick turned his attention back to their conversation.

"And I still brought home just about any injured animal I found. But I think she felt better about telling me I couldn't keep them since I already had a pet."

Her gaze wide and innocent, Darcy asked, "Have you, I don't know, ever thought about getting Maddie a puppy?"

"Oh, nice," he deadpanned. "Very subtle."

"Okay, okay, so my motives aren't entirely selfless. But look at them, Nick!"

Advertising agencies struck gold by putting kids and puppies in commercials. Nothing could be any cuter or bring out the warm fuzzies faster. "I always pictured having pets around when Maddie was growing up," he admitted.

But Carol hadn't wanted pets. As a stressed-out mother of a newborn and then active toddler, she'd sworn she couldn't handle one more thing. And Nick had agreed. He'd sensed from the beginning that his wife saw taking care of Maddie as more of a chore than a joy. It was hard work, he'd never once argued with her about that, but he hadn't understood how Carol could experience Maddie's first smile, first tooth, first step and not be blown away by the sheer wonder and love the way he was. And then when she left...

Well, Nick would readily admit he'd been too overwhelmed to consider taking on a new pet. He'd struggled through that first year, desperate to maintain a sense of normalcy even as his and Maddie's world was falling apart.

And then somewhere along the way, one year had turned to two and then three... Now five years had passed and Nick was still trying to keep their little world from changing. But the truth was, Maddie was growing up whether he wanted her to or not.

"I think you might be right," he told Darcy. "Not that my motives are completely unselfish, either. It's been a long time since I've heard Maddie laugh like that."

She tilted her head, quietly studying him with such intensity, he wondered if she could see right inside to the broken and missing pieces he'd patched together after his divorce. "When was the last time," she asked finally, "that you laughed like that?"

"Like an eight-year-old girl?"

"Funny! See, I knew you had a sense of humor. But when was the last time you let go and let yourself have some fun?"

Aah, now that he could give an answer to. After making a production of looking at his watch, he leaned close and murmured, "Two hours ago. On my parents' front porch swing."

Watching the soft color bloom in her cheeks and those knowing emerald eyes darken with desire, Nick longed to pull her back into his arms, to finish what they'd started on that front porch swing. "Want to know about the time before that?"

Her elegant throat moved as she swallowed, and a vivid memory replayed of him pressing his lips to that very spot. "I think I already know all about that," she whispered.

If they'd been alone—

But Maddie's laughter rang out once more, reminding him that they weren't alone.

Stepping back, he took a deep breath of air free of Darcy's warm, feminine scent. "Hey, Maddie, Darcy's had a long day, and I think it's time for the puppies to hit the sack, too."

"Oh, Daddy, do we have to go?"

The use of the cast-aside name hit Nick in the heart and refused to let go. He'd be damned lucky to get out of there without promising his daughter all four of the puppies, and he knew it. The soft smile Darcy gave him told Nick she recognized a sucker when she saw one, too, and that moment, that shared moment of emotional intimacy, had his stomach taking a sudden plunge down to his boots before rebounding back up into his throat.

He wasn't sure how he kept his voice even as he said, "Yeah, kid, we have to."

Maddie gave the mama dog a final pat before pushing to her feet and grinning up at Darcy. "Thanks for letting me come see them, Darcy."

"You're welcome, sweetie. I know they liked seeing you."

As they stepped into the living room, Maddie glanced down the hall, taking note of some boxes stacked outside what Nick assumed was a bedroom. "What's all this?" she asked as she rushed over to check out the boxes and whatever else she could see through the open doorway.

"Maddie." Embarrassment filled his protest at his daughter's unabashed nosiness, but Darcy only laughed and followed her down the hall where she reached into the bedroom and turned on an overhead light.

"My dad never lets me leave stuff out all over like this." Maddie waved her arm, her eyes sparkling, as if the piles of boxes formed some kind of magical castle.

"Yes, well, I should be better about putting things away, but most of this is for my shop and until I get all my shelves set up and displays arranged, I'm not going to have any room for this stuff."

Nick could tell most of the boxes were recent arrivals, packages marked with shipping labels. But toward the back of the room, he saw some moving boxes, each one carefully labeled with a specific room so Darcy would know where the items inside were meant to go—assuming she ever unpacked.

My mom and I moved around a lot when I was growing up. I don't know how many places we fixed up before packing up again.

Nick supposed that moving-on part was that much easier

if you never bothered to unpack in the first place. "This is all product for your store?" he asked.

"Most of it. Some are my mother's belongings. Other boxes are things I haven't gotten to yet. I've been so busy with getting the store ready," she added as if sensing some unspoken criticism, "I haven't had time to give much attention to this place."

"Sure." Her words made sense, and he couldn't argue with how hard she'd been working. He'd seen that for himself. But the boxes still unnerved him.

"Aunt Sophia said you're having a big party at your store," Maddie said.

"A grand opening, yes." Determination filled her voice, but that unwavering statement wasn't enough to erase the worry from her eyes.

The reminder made Nick realize he hadn't volunteered his and his brothers' help, but before he had the chance Maddie jumped in. "Can we go? Please?"

"We'll see."

His daughter seemed to have anticipated his response and gave an expected sigh in return. As they stepped outside with Maddie rushing a few steps ahead and down the porch steps, Darcy murmured, "I realize it's not your thing, but you should let her come to the grand opening with Sophia. She'll have fun, I promise."

He didn't have any doubts about that. But when it came to how much time he wanted Darcy to spend with his daughter? Oh, yeah, doubts up to his eyeballs. Especially after seeing the stacks of boxes that reminded him too much of coming home and finding a moving company packing up all his wife's belongings.

"We'll see," he repeated.

He thought Darcy might argue, but instead she simply gave him a smile. One that was both knowing and a little bittersweet. As if she sensed what he was doing. Opening the door to let her in, but only by the slightest crack. Pulling her close, but not too close.

He hadn't been kidding on the front porch swing when he had told her he didn't know what he was doing. He figured in the last few minutes, he'd done a good job proving it.

Quickly sweeping her hair back into a ponytail, Darcy glanced at the clock by her bedside. She still couldn't believe she'd slept so late. Lying in bed until after nine o'clock was a luxury she couldn't afford, not when she still had so much work to do. As tired as she was yesterday, she'd anticipated dropping like a stone the minute her head hit the pillow. Unfortunately, her mind had other ideas.

Her thoughts had spun around memories from the night before. Nick's unexpected invitation. Sophia's pleasure at seeing her and Nick together. Vanessa Pirelli's warm welcome. The kisses she and Nick shared on the front porch swing...

With Maddie as a mini chaperone, Darcy hadn't expected a repeat performance on her front porch. But she'd longed for...something. A hint or promise that their first date wouldn't be their last.

But then she'd encouraged Nick to let Maddie come to the grand opening, and everything changed. His reaction had nothing to do with spending time at her shop, but instead was about Maddie spending time with *her*. And while she could understand and even appreciate how protective he was of his daughter, she couldn't help wondering if the walls he had up around them might be too high to climb.

She had already tried to scale her way into a man's carefully constructed world only to fall. Aaron had let her close enough to convince Darcy he trusted her completely, close enough for her to agree to marry him. But the minute she turned out to be someone who might damage all he truly held near and dear, he'd let her go without a second thought.

The loss had been hard, but she'd survived.

Caring for Nick, for Maddie, only to have him realize she was too big of a risk to take on… Darcy wasn't sure she'd bounce back from that as easily. Was starting over with Nick really such a good idea when she already had a preview of how things would end? They'd played the game backward, giving in to passion before truly getting to know each other, but even if they started at square one and took things slow, feeling their way through the usual steps of dating, maybe even falling in love, did she really believe Nick would find room for her in his life? That "just the two of us" could become the three of them? Or would she always be on the outside?

Her heart ached at the thought, but daylight wasn't giving her any of the answers she hadn't found during the night. Forcing aside her thoughts, she shoved her feet into her tennis shoes without bothering to untie the laces and headed for the kitchen for one more check on the mama dog and her puppies. She'd filled the food bowl first thing that morning, not that anyone would know it. As always, the shiny metal surface was licked clean.

"Better than any dishwasher," she murmured as she took a few steps closer than usual into the laundry room. Moving slowly, she knelt next to the dog. Without Nick by her side, her pulse started picking up speed, her nerves started tightening her stomach.

You're afraid of the past. Don't you think it's time to let go?

She sank her fingers into the dog's smooth silver fur, and like the night before, nothing happened. Nothing bad happened.

Was she letting her past with Aaron influence her feelings about Nick now? Bracing for a heartache that might never come?

A knock on the front door took her by surprise, but the dog instantly cocked its head to the side, ears pricked forward in anticipation. "It's Nick, isn't it?"

Almost as if understanding her words, the dog's tail beat against the floor in welcome, and Darcy laughed. "If I had a tail, I think I'd be wagging it, too."

Instead, she hurried to the front door, opening it before he had a chance to knock a second time. Faint sunlight streamed in along with a cool breeze carrying the distant hint of rain and mist off the ocean, but she barely noticed, too busy soaking in the sight of the man in front of her. It was crazy to feel so eager to see him when less than twelve hours had passed, but last night had ended too abruptly, leaving so much unfinished.

A feeling Nick seemed to echo as he took a step over her threshold and closed the door behind him. "There's something I forgot to say yesterday."

She blinked. "Oh, okay. What?" She probably sounded like an idiot, but her pulse was pounding too loudly in her ears for her to hear as Nick stepped closer.

Reaching up, he cupped her face in his hands and lowered his head, each move slow and deliberate, giving her plenty of time to protest, to duck away, to offer her cheek. Too much time, she thought, as she waited for his kiss.

"Darcy," he murmured.

"Yes?"

"I just wanted to tell you…good night."

And then, finally, he kissed her. The ending that had seemed so unfinished the night before came to a perfect conclusion as his lips parted over hers. Despite her worries, she opened to him, to his kiss, to his embrace, to everything he was willing to give. Her arms climbed around his neck, holding fast, but even that wasn't enough. She wanted to grab hold of his heart, the way he had hers, and never let go.

Her legs were as unsteady as her breathing, and she hoped he didn't step back anytime soon or she might simply slide to the floor. With his mouth still hovering just above hers, Darcy met the heat and desire in his gaze and said the only thing she could think of. "It's morning."

The corner of his mouth lifted in a grin and his lips brushed against hers in a seductive kind of Braille that she could feel the words he spoke. "Then I guess I should say *good morning.*"

If *good morning* was anything like *good night,* Darcy wasn't sure she'd survive. At least not with her clothes and senses still intact. But instead of kissing her again, he stepped back and glanced down to her tennis shoes and up again, leaving a shivery heat behind. "You're working on your shop today."

The words were more of a statement than a question, but Darcy nodded just the same, a little disappointed she couldn't play hooky and spend the day with Nick instead. "I am. I'll be working right up to the grand opening."

"Last night, I talked to my brothers about helping with the remodel." Sensing her coming protest, he said, "You said you'd dreamed about moving here, coming back to the small town where your mother grew up, right?" At her slightly confused nod, he added, "Then let me show you the best part about Clearville and how the people who live here are always ready to lend a hand." Reaching up, he cupped her face in his hands. "I know this dream belonged to you and your mother, but maybe one small part of it could include me and my brothers."

Fighting back tears, she joked, "Because the Pirelli boys

have always secretly wanted to be part of a beauty boutique."

"Always," he vowed with mock gravity.

For all the times they'd talked about moving back and opening the shop, Alanna had never once made an actual plan to do so. Never looked into making the dream a reality the way Darcy had.

And for the first time since moving to this small town, this was no longer about making her mother's dream come true. Not anymore. This was about her own dream and following her own heart. And her heart kept leading her straight to Nick.

Chapter Twelve

A week later, Nick stood with the rest of his family as Darcy took center stage in her newly refurbished shop. It had taken hard work and the effort of all Pirelli hands on deck, but they'd gotten it done.

The walls were painted a soft pink above the wainscoting and chair rail. Black floating shelves, filled with products on display, were staggered on the back wall behind the check-out area. The same beadboard paneling on the walls now wrapped the front of a cabinet, and a new counter, a piece of black granite Drew swore was leftover from another job, graced the top.

The built-in shelves Darcy loved so much had been repainted the same glossy white as the wainscoting, and the scuffed, poorly repaired floors now had a smooth, uniform finish without losing their original character.

They'd accomplished most of the work the previous weekend, leaving the final touches and decorating for

Darcy to arrange and rearrange during the week. Nick had helped with carting the many boxes from her house to the small storage room at the back of the shop, so he'd already seen the final result of all the time and effort. Wanting to thank his family for the help and support, Darcy had invited everyone for a pre–grand opening celebration.

"Thank you all so much," she said, her green eyes shining with tears. "I never could have done this without you."

It took every bit of willpower Nick had not to pull her into his arms, right then and there, in full view of his family, and kiss her. She'd worked as hard as he and his brothers, putting in an effort that amazed him and the rest of his family. Nothing could replace having her mother at her side to see her dream come to life, but Nick hoped having *his* family there might have been the next best thing.

As for him, he couldn't imagine anything better. Watching Darcy hold her own in light of Sam's somewhat relentless teasing. Seeing her consider Drew's advice without every losing track of her own vision. And noticing how she carefully included Maddie in all the work, assigning the job of painting to the young girl and then following along behind her to fix any missed spots or runny messes his daughter might have made without ever letting on what she was doing.

Watching the two of them together cracked open something inside Nick's heart. The emotions he'd locked away for the past five years spilled out as he realized what he should have known all along. Darcy fit. She might not have been born and raised in Clearville. And she wasn't the solid, serious, *boring* woman he'd had in mind, but she was everything he hadn't been looking for. A woman who could keep him from becoming too staid, too serious, too boring by bringing light and laughter to his life.

"I don't know how I can ever repay you," Darcy was saying.

Tears shimmered in her eyes, and she was so beautiful, she took his breath away. He'd almost, almost gotten used to her in the casual clothes she'd been wearing the past few days, brightly colored T-shirts and jeans that were not only paint-splattered but easily could have been painted *on* as they faithfully followed every curve. But tonight she was back in her city-girl wardrobe wearing a teal-green silk shirt that cuffed at her elbows and wide-legged black trousers. Her red hair tumbled over her shoulders, and he couldn't keep from remembering how it felt having those strands brush against his naked chest.

Swallowing, Nick forced himself to concentrate on what his younger brother was saying before he embarrassed himself in front of his family.

"You don't have to thank us." Drew shook his head, speaking the words for all of them, but then he stepped close to her to add something only Darcy could hear. Whatever it was brought a hint of pink to her already flushed face as she shot a glance his way.

Nick wasn't sure he wanted to know what his brother had said as Darcy's quiet response of "I'll do that" trailed like a seductive promise over his skin.

"Hey, I've got an idea," Sam broke in as he slapped Drew on the back. "Pizza for everyone—Darcy's buying."

"Sam!"

His family's uniform protest had no effect on the youngest Pirelli son. Holding out his hands in an innocent-man gesture, he argued, "She said she didn't know how to repay us."

Laughing, Darcy overrode the rest of their objections. "Yes, definitely. Dinner's on me!"

* * *

"I think you've been holding out on me," Darcy said as Nick walked with her up the gravel driveway to her porch. After the music and laughter that had filled the pizza parlor, she welcomed the quiet sounds of night. A rustle of wind in the trees. A chirp of a distant cricket. The rapid beat of her heart as they neared her front door.

"Holding out?"

"Here I thought you were this solid, dependable single father and instead it turns out you're some backroom, pool-hall hustler."

The sky was clear enough for Nick's smile to flash in the moonlight. "I haven't shot pool in years. I figured Drew and Sam would wipe the floor with me."

"I think someone's being modest. I kept waiting for you to say you could take them with one hand tied behind your back."

"Well, what was I supposed to do with you and Maddie egging me on? I couldn't afford to look bad in front of my girls."

She and Maddie had been his cheering section during the sibling competition that turned a little more heated once the younger Pirellis realized Nick wasn't the pushover they'd expected. "I almost feel bad for Sam. I really don't know how he's going to pay you that million bucks he owes."

"One point two," Nick corrected as they laughed over Sam's outrageous bets and subsequent seven-figure losses. "But what about you?"

"Me?"

"Yeah, you seemed to have some kind of secret handshake going on with Maddie. I saw the two of you earlier at the pizza place whispering in the corner over cream sodas."

Darcy turned to face him at the front door. The porch

light cast only a faint glow, but enough for her to search his gaze. As protective as he was of his daughter, she thought she might find some sign of worry or wariness that Maddie had singled her out at the pizza parlor. But what she saw lifted her heart until she thought she might float up off the ground.

Nick trusted her. With his daughter. The most precious gift he had to give.

"Darcy?"

She blinked quickly, trying to focus on what she and Maddie had talked about. "Maddie told me that she's a little worried about being a flower girl."

"My mom and Sophia figured she'd be thrilled to be in the wedding."

"She is excited, but she's also nervous about wearing a 'poofy marshmallow dress.'"

"Poofy marshmallow?"

"Her description, not mine," Darcy said though she had to admit, it was an accurate one. A few days ago, Sophia had shown her a picture of the dress she had ordered for Maddie. A little-girl version of the bridal gown, the dress was beautiful—a full-skirted, ruffled creation of white satin and lace with cap sleeves and a bow tied beneath the bodice.

"I've always thought the flower girl and ring bearer had more responsibility than anybody else in the wedding party. All those petals to scatter and trying to keep the rings on the pillow. Tough jobs for a couple kids. Especially with a church full of people watching."

"Maybe, but all of a sudden, Maddie's been totally into dressing up and worrying about hair and clothes and makeup."

"All of a sudden?" she prompted.

"I thought her interests changed after her last visit to

see Carol…but you think Maddie's only interested in that stuff because of the wedding?"

"It's possible."

Nick's chest expanded on a huge sigh, and the grin on his face had the power to light her world. "You don't know what a relief it is to find out that's at least part of what's been bugging her lately. I wish she'd said something sooner."

"Your whole family is so excited, I think it took someone not in the wedding party to realize she's having a hard time admitting she's nervous."

"Not just someone," he murmured.

You.

The unspoken compliment sent bubbles of happiness fizzing inside, but she tried to downplay her reaction. "Maddie also said she's worried about tripping on her way down the aisle and 'ruining everything.' I told her after your mother alters the dress, she should practice walking around, picturing herself tossing rose petals down the aisle. Hopefully once she's comfortable in the dress, she won't be so nervous about the wedding."

"That's a great idea. Thank you, Darcy."

"Hey, don't be thanking me yet. It's not like you're getting off scot-free. This is only a temporary reprieve. It won't be too long before Maddie's not only interested in hair and makeup and clothes, but boys and dating, too."

Nick closed his eyes and groaned. "Don't remind me. Forget gray hair, I'll be stark white by the time she's a teenager."

"I doubt that." Not when his hair was still so thick and dark she itched to sink her fingers into the silky strands. "And besides, that time is still years away. Certainly not something you have to worry about tonight."

"No," he agreed, his voice dipping slightly. "Not tonight."

Tonight Maddie was still a little girl. A little girl who was spending the night at her grandparents'.

Awareness of a night to themselves had colored the entire evening. It had been there every time their eyes met over the pepperoni pizza they'd shared with Maddie. Every time they cheered Maddie on as she played one video game after another. Every time Nick hit another amazing shot against one of his brothers.

Every moment had been leading to this one when they were finally alone.

"We said we'd take things slow," he said. Was it a reminder to her or to himself?

Either way, Darcy reached up on tiptoe and brushed her lips against his. "We will," she promised. "We have all night."

"That's not—"

Deepening the kiss, she cut off his words, and his groan of surrender signaled a triumph for them both. His arms pulled her tightly against him, and Darcy did what she'd been longing to do. She sank her hands into his dark hair, anchoring herself to his kiss as the world tilted beneath her feet.

Was she setting herself up for another fall? A harder fall as her feelings for Nick had grown even stronger over the past week? Maybe. But this chance to be with Nick was one she couldn't walk away from. Not when she…loved him?

Wings of panic beat against her chest, but there was no denying the overwhelming emotion. She loved Nick. Likely had from the first moment they stood together on this porch.

His devotion to his daughter, his dedication to his family, even his reluctance to open his heart and give love another shot. Because just like that little spot on Main Street had been empty and abandoned for so long so the space would be available for her, Darcy felt the same was true for Nick's heart. He may not have known it, he might still not know it, but he'd simply been waiting for her. The same way she'd been waiting her whole life to fall totally and completely in love with him.

She fumbled in her purse for her keys, drawing a deep laugh from Nick that vibrated from her lips to her toes and all points in between. "What?" she breathed against his lips.

"City girl."

"Huh?"

Lifting his head long enough to take the keys from her hand and unlock the door, he said, "No one locks their houses around here."

"Really?" she asked as she backed into the darkened living room. She heard the clatter of the key ring Nick tossed aside and let her purse fall to the floor as the door swung shut behind them.

"Really."

"Wish I'd known. We would have been inside that much faster."

"Slow, Darcy. We're going slow."

"Right. Slow…" Like the slow trail of his lips down her throat. The slow fall of her blouse from her shoulders. The slow glide of his palms down her thighs as he stripped away her slacks.

"Too slow," she protested, her breath catching at the lingering journey his hands made back up her body to curve his fingers around her breasts. The silk and lace of her bra was in the way, and she wanted it gone. Now. Along with all of Nick's clothes. But he made her wait as they inched down the narrow hallway to her bedroom until finally, finally he tipped her back onto the cool mattress and kissed her again.

His body was a warm, solid weight above her, but too many clothes were a barrier to the firm muscle and heated skin she wanted to feel against her own. She tugged his shirt from his jeans, running her hands from his hips to his shoulder blades. His body arched beneath her touch, and Darcy reveled in the heady rush of knowing he was as affected by this passion between them as she was. But now if she could only break through his control…

"Darcy," he groaned her name in a low warning as she ran her fingers around to the front of his body, down his chest with its covering of dark hair and the ribbed muscles of his stomach. He sucked in a breath at the teasing stroke, unintentionally giving her extra room to work on the button of his jeans.

He whispered her name again, pulling back far enough to meet her gaze. This time, her frantic movements not only slowed but stopped, spellbound by the heat and hunger in his eyes. She watched as he stripped away his clothes. Goose bumps rose as she waited, every nerve ending alive and aching for his touch. Her heart thundered as he stretched out over her. She gasped when he stripped away her bra and cupped her breast, his thumb brushing over her nipple. Her legs shifted restlessly against his as the heat of his mouth followed. She sank her hands into his dark hair and held him tightly as pleasure threatened to spin her out of control.

Her hips rose as he slipped off her panties, his heated, slightly rough hands an arousing contrast to the cool silk and satin whispering against her skin. Tremors racked her body as he stroked the heart of her, need building inside until she cried out his name. Answering her desperation, he caught her mouth with his as he slid between her thighs and stilled.

Moonlight spilled through the open curtains, giving enough pale glow for Darcy to make out Nick's rugged features in the intimate moment—the wide forehead, straight nose, strong, stubborn jaw and sensual mouth. But it was his expression she wished she could read better. Was the tenderness and emotion she saw no more than a reflection of her own feelings—or could Nick be falling for her, too?

The words pressed against her breastbone, but she held them back. It was too soon, wasn't it? Too much of a risk when she couldn't take them back if Nick didn't feel the same. So she kissed him instead only to realize it was already too late. All the words she didn't say, all the love she felt, poured into that kiss and into every touch.

I love you…I love you…I love you…

Her pulse pounded a new three-beat rhythm, one she feared he was sure to feel for himself as he pressed his lips to the side of her neck and began to move. Each thrust matched the tempo of her rising emotions until she couldn't hold back any longer. The pleasure broke over her, pulling Nick with her into a final pulsating shudder.

Once their heartbeats and breathing slowed, Nick rolled to his back and brought Darcy to settle at his side. "Next time," he murmured, "we'll go slow."

The promise of a next time made Darcy smile, and as she drifted off to sleep, she knew this was what she'd been looking for. In the safety and comfort of Nick's arms, she'd finally found what it meant to be home.

If a more perfect morning was possible, Nick couldn't imagine it. Waking up with a beautiful woman… Waking up and making love to a beautiful woman…

What could be better? he wondered as he slipped from

the bed. Darcy murmured a protest, her hand smoothing over the now empty sheets, but she didn't wake. He smiled, watching her as he pulled on the jeans he'd discarded the night before. Her red hair spread out over the pillow, a deep, rich contrast to the white cotton and her own fair skin.

He itched to run his hands through the tempting locks one more time, but if he did, all that gorgeous hair and gorgeous skin would have him back in that bed again, and he'd already made the decision to let Darcy sleep.

She'd had a long week followed by a long night. Granted, they'd spent most of that time in bed, but neither of them had gotten much rest. And with her grand opening the following day, he figured she'd be too wired to sleep tonight.

So, cold shower and hot coffee for him and sleep for Darcy.

Twenty minutes later, he'd showered, taken care of the mama dog and her puppies, and had a pot brewing in the coffeemaker. His question from earlier that morning drifted through his thoughts. What could be better than waking up with a warm, wonderful, loving woman in his arms in the morning?

Waking up with Darcy in his arms *every* morning.

The answer should have hit him like a freight train out of the blue and yet it felt so…right. As perfect as that morning. He loved her. He was in love with Darcy Dawson. This wasn't about having a fling or diving into the fire until the flame burned out. It was so much deeper than that, so much purer and more permanent.

This was love. He swallowed hard. This was forever.

The sudden ring of his phone jarred Nick from his thoughts—a sharp, shrill sound he instantly recognized. He swore at the intrusion, tempted to let the call go to his voice mail. He let the phone ring a few times more as he slipped outside. Already knowing he was going to regret it, he hit a button on the phone and said, "Hello, Carol."

"Nick. How have you been?" His ex-wife's voice was as smooth as glass and, at times, her words were just as sharp. "Did you get the pictures I sent from Maddie's visit?"

"I did." Nick had already heard from Maddie what a great time she'd had. He hadn't really needed the visual proof. But because his daughter enjoyed looking through the photos, he added, "Thanks for sending them."

"She had a really great time. I hope you could see that."

"It was a good trip. A good vacation," he stressed because that's all it was. All Maddie's relationship with Carol ever would be.

His bad-luck feeling that his ex was up to something reared its ugly head again, but Nick was ready. He'd sensed Carol was up to something for weeks now. He hadn't pressed because time was on his side. Once Maddie was back in school, he could legitimately turn down any extra visits Carol requested. It would be too late for another trip, and Carol would have to wait until fall and Maddie's next scheduled visit.

"She's getting older, Nick. She—she needs me more now."

She needed you when she was three and afraid of the dark and crying for her mother! The accusations beat inside his skull, raging to get out, but Nick kept his mouth shut. He'd struggled through those first painful months when his daughter's unanswered cries had torn out his heart, but they'd gotten through it.

"She's gotten older each year. It happens. Maddie will be fine."

"You're so sure of that, aren't you? So sure you know best?"

"I'm not doing this again, Carol. I'm not extending Maddie's next visit."

"That's not why I called. This— This isn't about me, Nick."

Not about Carol. *Yeah, right.*

A long silence filled the line before his ex spoke again. "Besides, I would have thought you might want to send Maddie to me again. That way, you could have more time to be with your new girlfriend."

He should have seen it coming, but somehow the blow was one hundred percent unexpected.

"Not exactly keeping up with your end of the bargain, are you, Nick? Didn't we both decide to keep Maddie away from our casual affairs?"

"Darcy's not—"

He cut the words off before he could argue that what he had with Darcy was anything but a casual fling. There was nothing casual about his feelings for her, but did he really have any idea of her feelings?

For all the time they'd spent together—talking, laughing, making love—none of their plans ever crept beyond a day or two ahead. Why was that? Because they were still taking advantage of the present, as Darcy had talked about that night in her kitchen? Or because she didn't see them having a future?

Nick hated the doubts and uncertainty that clawed at him, tearing apart the fragile connections he and Darcy had made. He'd been so certain once. Confident and without a single doubt that his dreams could become Carol's dreams. And he'd been so wrong.

"Darcy's not what, Nick?"

"She's none of your business."

"You made her my business when you brought her around our daughter."

You made her my business...

A chill raked down his spine at the unspoken threat behind those words. "What do you want, Carol?"

"I have a job opportunity. A chance to fill in for another manager who's taken a four-month medical leave. The hotel is in Paris."

Déjà vu sucked him into the past—Carol informing him of the transfer that would have taken her to New Orleans. His nearly desperate attempts to convince her to stay.

"Paris... Well, congratulations."

"I haven't accepted the job yet."

"Why not?"

"Why not?" Righteous indignation clipped her words. "Because of Maddie, Nick."

"I guess you have another choice to make—stay or go." Carol could pretend to debate her options all she wanted, but he already knew how this story ended. "But there's no way I'm putting Maddie on a plane to visit you in Paris."

"I wasn't thinking about having her visit. This is a tremendous opportunity for her, Nick."

"What the hell are you talking about?"

"Living in Europe! I could hire a tutor for her. It would be a chance for her to see the world—"

"No way."

"You won't even think about it?"

Think about his daughter living thousands of miles away for four months? Cold sweat broke out on the back of his neck. "Forget it, Carol."

"Just because you want to limit your life to a five-mile radius from where you were born doesn't mean Maddie should be stuck there, too! There's more to life than small-town Clearville, Nick." Carol took a deep breath, a sure sign she was pulling out the big guns. "Why not ask Maddie what she wants?"

* * *

By the time Darcy opened her eyes, morning sunlight streamed through the windows and across the bed. The sheets beside her were empty, but the scent of coffee drifted down the hall.

Nick was still there.

The warmth and brightness outside matched how she felt inside, and as she met her expression in the mirror ten minutes later, she was still smiling. A quick, hot shower had brought a flush to her skin, but the spark in her eyes was solely thanks to the man in her kitchen. She dressed quickly, layering green and white tank tops over a white peasant-style skirt and pulling back her hair into a high ponytail.

Nick was standing at the sink with his back to her as she walked in the kitchen. Just the sight of his dark hair, broad shoulders and long, jean-clad legs had her heartbeat picking up speed—that same beat from the night before still going strong.

I love you, she thought, but before she had a chance to show him, to wrap her arms around his waist and lean in for a good-morning kiss, he turned. Rising up on tiptoe, she brushed her lips against his.

"Good morning." When he didn't respond, she sank back on her heels as a feeling of dread slid down her spine and pooled in her stomach.

He gestured to the pot on the counter. "Seems like it's my turn to offer you a cup of coffee," he said, but his smile didn't reach his eyes.

"Thanks." She took the mug he poured only to set it aside, knowing the hot liquid would never get past the lump in her throat.

"I, um, need to get going. I have to go pick up Maddie."

Something flashed in his eyes at his daughter's name, a

combination of pain and panic, and Darcy quickly offered, "I could go with you."

But he was already shaking his head. "I don't— I can't—"

Desperation pushed at her and she started talking over the words she feared he was going to say. "I thought we could come back here, and she could see the puppies again. It's been a few days, and you know how fast they're growing."

"Darcy, stop! Please." Nick closed his eyes for a second, exhaling a breath that left his shoulders bowed beneath a weight heavy enough to break him.

She swallowed. "Don't. Don't do this, Nick. Don't shut me out again. Can't you see I'm not trying to take any part of Maddie from you?"

Turning away from her, he gripped the edge of the sink, the muscles in his arms standing out in sharp relief. "I know that."

Her heart ached and each word she spoke scraped against the growing knot of tears. "I just want to be a part of your life—yours and Maddie's. I thought that was what you wanted, too."

"I— It doesn't matter what I want."

"How can it not matter?" How could everything they'd shared over the past few days—the time they'd spent talking and laughing, the time she'd spent *falling in love*—suddenly not matter? "Did I do something wrong?"

The confusion on Nick's face answered her question before he did. "No. No, it's not you. You didn't do anything."

So was that it? The old "it's not you, it's me" speech? Fighting the sting of tears, she said, "I just don't understand."

"It's…Carol."

That wasn't the answer she expected. "Your ex-wife?"

"She called this morning. She knows about us."

Darcy swallowed hard, but the lump that formed at his words remained lodged firmly in her throat. *She knows about us...*

"I didn't realize our relationship was supposed to be a secret." Something to be hidden away, out of sight, a dirty little secret like one her father had kept from his real family all these years—the daughter he never acknowledged.

"It's not."

"Then what difference does it make if she knows?"

"You're the first woman I've...dated since the divorce."

At another time, Darcy might have been happy to hear she was the first woman Nick had let back into his life. But not now. Not when the words sounded almost like an accusation. "Is she upset that we're together? Is that what this is about?"

"Carol doesn't get *upset*. She seems to think that since I'm so busy with my new girlfriend, I won't mind if she takes Maddie to Paris for the rest of the year."

"What?"

After listening to Nick repeat the details from the phone call—Carol's job offer and insistence that Maddie make the decision about whether to move with her to Paris—Darcy asked, "Are you going to talk to Maddie about going?"

"There's no reason to talk to her because there's no way I'm letting her go to France for four months!"

"Not for four months. But what about fall break? She's already scheduled to see Carol then, right?"

"In San Francisco. Not Paris!" He flung out an arm, the back of his hand overturning his mug. He swore as the hot coffee splashed over his hand. His anger creeping away as quickly as it had reared its head, he gave another sigh. "Look, maybe with all the moving around you do, this doesn't seem like a big deal, but to me it is."

Darcy paused before slowly stating, "No, I think I get it." And she was starting to see more than she wanted to.

All the moving around you do. Present tense, as if her move to Clearville was temporary. As if their relationship was nothing more than temporary.

A dishtowel hung over the oven handle and they reached for it at the same time, their fingers brushing against cool cotton and warm skin—hers dry and soft, his damp and slightly rough. Darcy quickly dropped her hand and stepped out of Nick's way.

Throwing in the towel, she thought inanely because it was happening again.

She'd become a liability, a danger to his future, and like Aaron, Nick was cutting his losses and tossing her aside. But she had to try one more time to make him see what they had was worth fighting for and that their feelings for each other made them stronger, not weaker.

"You should talk to Maddie about Paris, Nick. She loves you, and Clearville is her home. Just…tell her how you feel."

She looked into his dark eyes, reading all the doubt and uncertainty in his tortured gaze, and wondered if he could see all the hope and hurt that was surely written in hers.

I love you, Nick, and my home and my heart are with you now. Tell me you feel something.

But he kept silent, and Darcy could see he'd made up his mind. About Maddie. About them.

"Not every woman you love is going to leave you, Nick."

But when he didn't look at her, when he didn't ask her not to leave, that was exactly what Darcy did. Turning, she walked out of the kitchen, the sunlight that had seemed so welcoming only moments before now casting a painful glare. "You can let yourself out, Nick. We both know you already know the way."

Chapter Thirteen

"I can't believe you're not going to Darcy's grand opening," Sophia said as she stormed inside the house the minute Nick opened his front door. "After helping get the place ready, being there for Darcy the whole way, you're going to bail on her now?"

Nick closed the door behind his sister with a little more force than necessary. Never in all his life had he bailed on someone he loved.

And he loved Darcy.

The realization stole over him once more, draining away his anger and leaving behind only the empty ache of loss. He'd never planned on falling in love again, not after the mistakes he'd made with Carol. But at least his failed marriage had given him Maddie. How could he take the risk of following his heart now when this time it could cost him his daughter?

"Don't you think I want to go?" he demanded of his little sister. "Don't you think I want to be there for Darcy?"

"Then why aren't you coming with us?"

He'd agreed, reluctantly, to let Maddie go with Sophia to the celebration, but he couldn't do it. He couldn't be with Darcy, knowing they couldn't be together.

Dogging his heels as he stalked into the kitchen, Sophia asked, "What's going on, Nick?"

Opening the refrigerator, he bent down to grab two bottles of water. When he straightened, he nearly bumped into his sister, who was standing between the refrigerator and the granite island, blocking his path out of the kitchen. She'd always been on the small side while growing up and she was still petite, especially compared to the Pirelli men and her future husband. But with her arms crossed over her growing belly and her dark eyes flashing, Sophia made it clear she wasn't going anywhere until she had the answers she was looking for.

Nick didn't know how or when their roles had changed—from Sophia being the bratty little sister and him being the older, wiser brother to Sophia now having the answers while he floundered somewhat cluelessly. And while he might not like it, he could use whatever help he could get.

He handed her one of the water bottles before opening and draining half of his own, wishing with each swallow that it was something stronger. Something that would make the next words easier to say. The plastic crackled in his hand as he set the bottle aside. "Carol called. She has a temporary job offer in Paris."

"Wow, Paris," Sophia breathed, thoughts of the City of Light bringing a sparkle to her dark eyes.

"You could try not to sound so impressed."

"Sorry, but it is a big deal. And why would you care if Carol goes to France?"

"She wants Maddie to go with her."

After filling Sophia in on the conversation, including his ex's pointed comment about making Darcy her business, Nick added, "I didn't realize the Clearville grapevine stretched all the way to San Francisco."

His sister was silent for a moment, that knowing and somewhat pitying look back in her eyes.

"What?" he prodded.

"If you're looking for the source of the leak, you might want to check with your own daughter. Maddie might not realize you and Darcy are together, but I'm sure she's talked about all the time you've been spending together lately Carol's bound to have connected the dots."

Maddie. Of course. Why hadn't he thought of that?

"But you think Carol finding out about Darcy has something to do with this?"

"Not the job offer itself, but definitely wanting to take Maddie for four months. That's longer than all her visitations for the past three years combined! I can't believe it's a coincidence."

"Let's say you're right. Maybe your relationship with Darcy pissed Carol off. So what? You and Darcy have a real chance to be happy together. Fight for that chance!"

"But this isn't just about me and Darcy! I have to think about Maddie, too. What happens if I turn our lives upside down, if I stir up this hornet's nest with Carol, and in the end Darcy walks away? I don't think I could handle that, Sophia."

"Let's talk about Carol first and then we'll move on to how much of a bonehead you're being about Darcy. No one is ever going to question how much you love Maddie. Everyone knows how much she means to you—including your ex-wife. Unfortunately, she's not above using how you feel to get her own way."

He wasn't unaware of his ex-wife's ability to manipulate him. "Carol's always been good at hitting where it hurts. She knows my love for Maddie is my biggest weakness."

Setting down her water bottle, Sophia reached out and grabbed his hands. "That's where you're wrong, Nick. Where you've always been wrong. Love isn't a weakness. It's your greatest strength. It's where you turn when times go bad. What you hold on to when everything else slips away. Not trusting in love...*that's* what makes you vulnerable."

Could Sophia be right? His fear of Maddie changing, of the two of them growing apart, had been a big factor in his decision to try to find the right kind of woman. His criteria for the role scrolled through his thoughts just like they had that first night on his way to Darcy's house. Someone with Clearville roots who could be a constant, consistent, solid presence.

A woman, he was now ready to admit, who wouldn't challenge him or excite him or tempt him to risk his heart.

He wasn't about to share *that* boneheaded idea with his sister.

"Have you talked to Maddie about going to Paris?" One look at Nick's expression had Sophia shaking her head. "Of course not. Just like you haven't bothered to tell Darcy how you feel, either."

"I don't know if I can do this, Sophia," he confessed, sinking onto one of the bar stools at the island. "To try to make a place for Darcy in my life when most days I feel like I barely have a handle on being a single parent."

"You don't need to make a place for Darcy, Nick. The spot's already there, just waiting for her. The question is whether or not you'll let her in instead of trying to keep her at some safe distance where she doesn't belong."

That was exactly what Darcy had accused him of doing,

wasn't it? Keeping her on the edge of his and Maddie's life. Not truly letting her inside.

Pushing off the stool as if he could leave his thoughts behind so easily, he said, "I'll go get Maddie. She's not going to want to miss any of the grand opening."

Sophia let him leave but not without a final piece of advice. "You're the one who's missing out, Nick, and if you let Darcy go, you're going to regret it."

With her words following him down the hall, he gave a quick knock on Maddie's open bedroom door. "Maddie." He glanced inside in time to see her stuff something beneath her pillow. Ignoring the furtive action, he said, "Your aunt Sophia is here. Are you ready to go?"

She hopped off the bed without meeting his gaze. "Yep. All ready."

"Okay, but is there something you want to tell me first?"

Maddie chewed on her lower lip for a moment before blurting out, "I think you should come with us! You'll hurt Darcy's feelings if you're not there, and it's not nice to hurt people's feelings."

He blinked, taken aback by his daughter's unexpected scolding. *You'll hurt Darcy's feelings....*

Too late for that. He'd seen the pain in her gaze yesterday when he hadn't stopped her from walking away.

Not every woman you love is going to leave....

"That's not what I meant, Maddie. Do you want to tell me what you're hiding under your pillow?"

Guilt flickered in her blue eyes as she reached over and pulled out the small crimson-colored sachet. It was one Darcy had given Maddie as a thank-you for the work she had done. As he sank down onto the bed beside Maddie, the spicy scent drifted toward him along with a wealth of memories—of his ex-wife. Carol used to decorate the house with bowls of potpourri. Bits of bark and pinecones that always smelled of cinnamon.

Was that why Maddie had picked that particular sachet? Because it reminded her of Carol? Nick swallowed. Did Maddie miss her mother that much?

"You know, cinnamon is your mother's favorite. I remember when our house used to smell just like this."

"That's how her condo in San Francisco smells," Maddie admitted, her voice soft.

"Maddie, I know how much you miss your mother—"

"I do!" she broke in, her blue eyes swimming with tears. "I do miss her!"

The fissure in his heart felt big enough to hold all the water in the Atlantic, but Nick forced himself to nod. He'd always said he would do whatever was best for Maddie. If that meant letting her go, handing her over to Carol and allowing the two of them to move to Paris for the longest four months of his life, then that was what he would have to do. But before he could tell Maddie about her mother's job offer, the little girl picked up the sachet, squeezing it hard between both hands.

"Mommy says she misses me *all* the time and she thinks about me *every* day."

A hint of desperation in his daughter's voice cut through Nick's despair, and he stopped to listen to what Maddie was saying and to the force behind her words. Was this about how much Maddie missed Carol…or about how much *Carol* missed Maddie?

His daughter's words sounded all too much like his own conversations with Carol—verbal battles where everything, even missing their daughter, turned into some kind of competition.

His ex excelled at that kind of manipulation, and that she'd try to *guilt* Maddie into missing her made his blood boil. It took everything he had not to charge out of Maddie's room, get Carol on the phone and tell her exactly what he thought of the games she was playing. He was that angry, that furious…that scared.

Sophia was right; he'd always seen love as a weakness, something that could be exploited, something that would eventually cause him pain. He was afraid of losing Maddie, of losing Darcy. Afraid, even, that Carol had been right, that the failure of their marriage had been all his fault and that he was destined to make those same mistakes again.

"Maddie, you love your mother and she loves you," he said, knowing that was true even if Carol didn't always make the right choices in showing that love. "If some days you miss her, that's okay. And if other days, you're busy with friends or school, and you don't miss her as much, that's okay, too. And I want you to know you can talk to me about how you're feeling. Even if you're sad or angry about how much you miss her. Okay?"

Eyes still downcast, his daughter nodded. "Sometimes… Sometimes I wish—"

Taking a breath, he braced for the words he never wanted to hear, for Maddie's plea to go live with Carol. *Love is your greatest strength.* He hoped to God his little sister knew what she was talking about, but it was going to take more strength than he thought he had to let his daughter walk out of his life.

"Sometimes I wish Mommy still lived here."

"Here? In Clearville?"

She nodded. "That way I wouldn't miss her and she wouldn't have to miss me because we could be together."

"But, Maddie—"

Jumping off the bed, she stuck the sachet back under her pillow. "She lives in San Francisco now. That's where her home is and her friends and her job…"

As she repeated that list by rote, Nick realized this was a conversation she'd had before—with Carol. And for a split second he actually felt sorry for his ex, realizing it must have been much harder for Carol to turn down Maddie's request for her to come back home than it ever had been for her to turn down his.

"Actually, sweetheart, there's something I want to talk to you about." Waiting until she'd sat back down on the bed beside him, he said, "Your mother has a chance to go work in Paris for the next few months and—" he cleared his throat around the lump lodged there "—she wants you to go with her."

Her eyes widening, she exclaimed, "But that's in, like, another country!"

"Yeah." He gave a short laugh as if that might somehow release the pressure building inside his chest. "France is another country. But you could stay there with your mom and—"

"No! I don't want to go. This is my home. Where my friends and my school are. And you and Grandma and Grandpa and—"

As his daughter went on with their list of family members, Nick pulled her into his lap, holding tight and knowing his fears had been for nothing. No matter what the future held, she would always be with him because love would keep them close. "I love you, Maddie."

"I love you, too, Daddy. Please don't make me go."

"Sweetheart, I don't want you to go anywhere. You know that. But I thought maybe you would want to." Jiggling her on his lap, he said, "You know how boring it can be around here sometimes."

"Sometimes," she admitted, "but not anymore."

He nodded. "I know you like hanging out with the puppies and helping at Darcy's store."

"I do, but I think you like Darcy even more."

"Me?"

She nodded, her soft, silky hair brushing his chin with the scent of strawberry shampoo. "You laugh a lot when she's around, and I like it when you're happy."

"Yeah, I like that, too. So, you really think I should go to the grand opening?"

Maddie bounced out of his arms, her childish energy making it impossible for her to stay close for long, but that was okay. "You have to come! Darcy will be so excited to see you."

Wishing he had a fraction of her certainty, he murmured, "I hope you're right, kiddo."

Darcy had expected the grand opening of her store to be bittersweet. To see her mother's dream come true without being able to share it with her was bound to break her heart a little. And it did. But looking around her crowded boutique as the women of Clearville spritzed and sprayed and tested the perfumes and lotions and makeup she had on display, it wasn't thoughts of her mother that hit Darcy out of the blue or brought the burn of tears to her eyes.

It was Nick.

She couldn't turn around without bumping into memories. From the recent days they'd spent with his brothers, working to get the place ready for tonight, to the day he snatched her off the ladder, to the first time he kissed her. Thoughts of him were everywhere, and each time the bell rang, she glanced at the door, hoping he would show.

"Darcy!" Sophia's excited greeting snapped Darcy back into focus as the pregnant brunette gave her a quick hug. "This turnout is amazing! But I knew it would be. You're going to be a smashing success."

"Thanks for the encouragement. I know a lot of this is curiosity about a new place in town—"

"But your products are going to keep shoppers coming back for more."

"I hope so. I've dreamed about this for so long...." It was what she and her mother had always talked about—a place of their own in a town they could call home. And maybe there'd been a time when that would have been enough. But now Darcy wanted more.

As if reading her thoughts, Sophia lowered her voice. "My brother's an idiot, but don't give up on him just yet."

As much as she longed to take her friend's advice to heart, Darcy wasn't the one who'd given up. Nick had. She'd become a risk he wasn't willing to take and she had yet to tell him about the scandal surrounding her birth. If she told him the whole story, did she really think Nick with his reluctance to start any kind of relationship would react any better than Aaron had?

Another shopper asked a question, and after that, she managed to keep her head, if not her heart, focused on her reason for moving to Clearville in the first place.

Darcy wasn't sure how many shoppers she greeted or free samples she handed out before she noticed a curvy blonde debating over the scented candles displayed on one of the round tables at the front of the shop. She'd been in Debbie Mattson's bakery only a few times, but Darcy recognized the other woman, who gave a friendly smile as their gazes met. "Hi, I'm Darcy Dawson."

"Plain bagel with low-fat cream cheese," the baker added, naming the order Darcy had placed a few weeks ago. "Occupational hazard. I might not remember a name, but I never forget an order."

"Well, you're right. Darcy Dawson, low-fat bagel," she

said, foolishly wishing she'd ordered something a little more sophisticated, like a croissant or an éclair.

"Sophia told me this place was going to be great, and now I see why she was so excited."

"She's been very supportive since I moved here. I haven't known her long, but I already consider her a good friend."

"She's great. So is her whole family, but I'm guessing you already know that," Debbie said with a sly glance. "Nick's needed someone like you to shake up his world for a long time."

After the way she and Nick had left things, Darcy didn't share the other woman's confidence. Rearranging the candles on the pink-cloth-covered tables—groups of two, groups of three, a single, solitary row—she said, "I'm not so sure."

"Well, I am. I've known Nick my whole life, so trust me on this."

"Were you and Nick ever…involved?"

Debbie's laughter was too genuine to be anything but honest. "No. I've never had a thing for any of the Pirelli brothers. Well, unless you count the time Sam kissed me on the playground, but Sam kissed all the girls. And I mean *all* the girls. The three of them are like family. Dating one of them would be like dating my cousins—no mystery, no surprises." Her eyes locked over Darcy's shoulder and she murmured, "Speaking of surprises…"

She turned in time to see Nick and Maddie walk in, each of them carrying a single red rose. Her pulse pounding, Darcy focused on Maddie because she thought it would be easier, safer, than looking at the little girl's father. But then she saw Maddie's bright smile and the pink T-shirt and black leggings she wore because those were the colors of *her* shop, and Darcy felt her heart break all over again. She'd fallen for Nick's daughter as hard as she'd fallen for Nick.

Father and daughter stopped right in front of her, and Darcy had no choice but to raise her gaze to meet Nick's. Dressed in a pair of khaki pants and a denim shirt roll-cuffed to reveal tanned, muscular forearms, he looked gorgeous in a casual, unpretentiously masculine way. As the only man to have crossed the threshold to her shop since the doors opened, he should have looked out of place, but if he felt that way at all, it didn't show in the confident strides he'd taken in her direction.

"Darcy! We brought you flowers!" Maddie announced, holding out the rose for her to take and then wrapping her arms around Darcy's waist in a hug the minute they were free. Gazing up at her from beneath her dark bangs, the little girl said, "Your store looks so beautiful."

"Thank you, Maddie. But it's all because of you and your family." Tapping the little girl on her freckled nose with the rosebud, she said, "I couldn't have done it without you."

"Hey, Maddie, I see your aunt Sophia over there, and I know she's just dying to buy you some makeup."

A huge grin lit her face at her father's words. "Makeup, Daddy, really?"

"Really. Go check it out."

The little girl didn't have to be told twice, sprinting off to the other side of the store, leaving Nick and Darcy alone. Or as alone as two people could be in a room full of curious people. "Makeup, Nick, really?"

"Sophia promised she'd find some kind of clear lip gloss and some pink nail polish and I told Maddie it would only be for special occasions… And I've just opened Pandora's box, haven't I?"

"Pretty much, but it was bound to happen sooner or

later." The smile she'd been clinging to faded away as she admitted, "I wasn't sure you'd come."

"Maddie wanted to. *I* wanted to. Congratulations. It looks like you have a huge success on your hands."

"It's just a start."

"You'll make it work."

If only he had that kind of confidence in the two of them, Darcy wished, only to see something new in his dark eyes. Something different. Something that made her blood course a little faster in her veins with a hope she was afraid to feel.

"I know you've got a full house here, but I'd like to talk later."

"It seems like you said everything you had to say a few days ago." Darcy had to give Nick credit. He didn't flinch away from the accusation. His gaze stayed locked on hers long enough for her to see the deep regret. "Nothing's changed since then."

"That's where you're wrong. Things have changed. I've changed."

Her scoffing laugh barely disguised the sob building in her chest. "Just like that? I'm supposed to believe it was that easy?"

"No!" Nick's exclamation caught the attention of the closest shoppers, and both Sophia and Maddie looked over with concern. Lowering his voice, he added, "I've spent the past few days facing what my life would be like without you. Believe me, there was nothing easy about it."

His gruff words went straight to her heart. She'd faced that same emptiness, that same loneliness. It wasn't easy. But she couldn't help thinking that maybe it was easier. Easier to end their relationship now than to end it weeks or months from now.

"If you'll just give me a second—" He winced and

amended, "Third chance, I'll prove it to you. I'll spend my life proving it to you."

Darcy's breath caught. He wasn't saying what she thought he was saying. He couldn't be. And yet the certainty and conviction on his handsome face left no room for doubt. "I can't— I can't do this right now." She glanced around through blurry eyes, feeling as if the whole place was focused on her. "A group of us is going over to The Bar and Grille later to celebrate. If you want to talk then…"

"I'll be there," Nick promised.

Darcy nodded and crossed her arms over the nerves clawing at her stomach. She knew Nick would show. The only question was how long would he stick around once she told him the truth about her past?

Chapter Fourteen

Nick had walked into The Bar and Grille with a plan, but like most of his plans, things weren't working out the way he'd hoped. His goal had been to sweep Darcy onto the darkened dance floor the moment she stepped through the old-fashioned swinging doors. Holding her close while the band played would give him the privacy he needed to tell her about his conversation with Maddie as well as the call he'd made to Carol.

It would also give him the chance to take her into his arms and tell her he loved her.

But a crowd had gathered as he waited for her to arrive, and by the time she did, it seemed half the people inside had simply followed her from her grand opening to the bar, and she was surrounded by well-wishers and friends alike.

This was her night, her big moment, and Nick didn't want to take that away from her. He wanted her to enjoy herself, to have fun, to— Oh, who was he trying to kid?

He wanted to steal her away, big moment or not, so he wouldn't have to share her with the circle of people crowding around her.

"Hey, Nick." Dragging his gaze away from Darcy and her admirers, he glanced up in time to watch Debbie slide into the empty seat across from him. "You okay?"

Realizing he was strangling his beer bottle in a death grip, he forced himself to relax and take a swallow. "Fine. Great," he said as he met Debbie's disbelieving gaze. "You know I never did thank you."

"Thank me?"

"For the piña colada cake. For knowing what I didn't even know I wanted."

She grinned. "It's easy to get stuck in a rut. But all it takes is something—or *someone*—new to knock you right out of it."

Darcy had done more than knock him out of a rut. She'd righted his world and put him back on course. She'd saved him from a loveless future, and he'd nearly blown it. *Please don't let me have blown it.*

"Nick!" A hard slap to his back jarred him from his thoughts and announced Sam's arrival. "And if it isn't Little Debbie." Bending down, Sam kissed the blonde's cheek and flashed her a grin.

"Seriously, Sam. You've been calling me that since we were in grade school, and I wasn't *little* then, either."

"But you're still sweet."

Nick shook his head as his youngest brother swung around the chair next to Debbie and straddled it. If any other man even thought of using a line like that, he'd end up getting his face slapped, but Sam's teasing drew an instant smile from Debbie who, as everyone in town knew, could give as good as she got.

"And you're still full of it," she shot back as her gaze

drifted toward the dance floor. "You know, Will's a sweet-heart, but he's a killer on a good pair of shoes."

Following her wincing glance, Nick caught sight of his brother's young mechanic dancing with Darcy. In no time Will's heel landed squarely on Darcy's foot.

"Someone," Debbie said with a pointed stare at Nick, "should get off his butt and ask her to dance."

Trying hard not to limp thanks to her throbbing toes, Darcy smiled at the young mechanic. "Thanks for the dance, Will," she said. "I think I'll—"

"Dance with me."

The deep voice interrupted her ready excuse, and her aching feet suddenly stopped hurting. Darcy couldn't be certain they were even touching the ground as Will stepped away with a tip of his cap and Nick pulled her into his arms. After their very first step, Darcy knew she wouldn't have to worry about her feet anymore. But her heart... Oh, her heart was in serious danger.

A couple bumped Darcy from behind, sending her stumbling against Nick. The sudden, unexpected contact of her breasts against his chest, his thigh between hers, sent a rush of heat flooding her cheeks. Trying to blame her reaction on embarrassment at her clumsiness, she gave a shaky laugh as she regained her footing. "You saved me from Will, but who's going to save you from me?"

A weighted silence followed her teasing question, and Darcy looked up to meet Nick's gaze. "I've been asking myself that same question," he said.

Darcy's feet were solidly beneath her once again, but that didn't keep her from feeling as though she were balanced on a razor's edge and just waiting to fall. "And?" she asked softly.

"Turns out I don't need to be saved from you. I've already been saved by you."

Her heart skipped a beat, but she wasn't ready to follow its lead. Not yet. She'd already been twice burned, and she found herself shying away from the fire in his eyes. She couldn't give in, couldn't trust what Nick was feeling until he knew everything. "Nick—"

"I talked to Maddie," he said, quickly overriding her unspoken protest. "She actually thinks I'm a pretty okay dad."

"I think we all know you're more than that."

"It's taken me awhile, but I think I've finally started to figure out there's more to parenting than responsibility. That loving Maddie doesn't mean holding on so tightly. Sometimes, it means letting go just a little and trusting in that love to keep her close."

Her eyes widened as she realized what his words meant. "You told her about Paris."

"You were right. She doesn't want to go. Clearville is her home, and she doesn't want to leave."

The happiness in his crooked smile went straight to her heart, and she couldn't help giving him a quick hug. "I'm so glad, Nick. But what about Carol? Has she dropped the idea of Maddie going with her?"

"No. Unfortunately, nothing to do with my ex-wife is ever that simple. Had Maddie wanted to go, of course, that would have been the end of it as far as Carol was concerned. But now that Maddie doesn't want to go, Carol's threatening to get the lawyers involved again."

"Oh, Nick."

"I know." His smile drifted away, replaced by a worried frown. "I can't believe we'll have to go through all of that again. Testifying in front of a judge. Asking my family to stand up as witnesses. Waiting for Carol to start slinging mud and trying to dig up dirt."

Dig up dirt.

The words echoed through Darcy's mind again and again. Oh, God. Why hadn't she thought something like this might happen?

Dig up dirt.

Aaron had worried her past might cost him in the court of public opinion when it came time for him to run for office, but what if her past came to light in a real court of law? What if she somehow cost Nick his daughter?

She stumbled, missing a step, and would have fallen if not for Nick's arms around her.

"Darcy, are you okay?"

They'd come to a stop in the middle of the dance floor, oblivious to the couples still swaying around them. "I can't— I can't do this, Nick."

"What are you talking about?"

"That night on your parents' porch, you asked me if it was too much. Well, this is. Judges. Testifying. Custody battles." Darcy shook her head. "It's not really what I signed up for. I mean, I thought we'd have a good time, have some fun, you know?"

Heart breaking, she watched as the cold mask slipped back in place on Nick's face. The relaxed, teasing man she'd fallen in love with over the past few days disappeared behind the remote stranger she'd first met. That he was building up the walls she'd tried so hard to break down, using the old shields against her, laid her heart open, but it was the only way. The only way she could protect what Nick valued most. If her past cost him his daughter, she'd never forgive herself.

"Fun, right… A couple of meaningless dates."

Hearing Nick repeat her words, lumping himself in with the likes of Travis Parker, a sob of denial clawed at her insides, frantically trying to break free. She had to go now. Had to end this. Now.

"I'm not the kind of woman you need." Laughter rang out from their table, and she glanced over where Debbie and Sam were still sitting. "You need—you need someone like Debbie." What had the other woman said earlier? No mystery, no secrets… That was the kind of woman who could testify in a courtroom and help Nick's cause.

"What are you talking about, Darcy? Debbie's a great girl and a great friend, but I don't need her. I don't love her! I love—"

Desperate to escape, she darted off the dance floor, squeezing past locked couples and shoving open the first door she saw. Cool air hit her heated face, chilling the tears she couldn't wipe away fast enough. Blinking rapidly, she came to a quick stop and swore. Instead of finding a back door, she'd trapped herself on an outdoor patio cordoned off with a wrought-iron railing.

She couldn't risk going back inside, couldn't face the hurt in Nick's dark eyes again without blurting out how much she loved him. Maybe if she waited, he would leave and she could sneak away like the pathetic coward she was.

Not until the acrid scent of cigarette smoke drifted toward her did Darcy realize she wasn't alone on the small patio. Glancing over her shoulder, she choked back a watery groan when she spotted Travis leaning against the building. Pushing away from the brick, he ground out his cigarette beneath his shoe before sauntering her way.

"Seems like things aren't working out too well with you and the doc."

Seeing the smug smile on his face, Darcy didn't bother to hold her tongue. "Still better than they worked out for you and me."

"That's only because you won't give me a chance."

"A chance to do what, Travis? Spread more lies about me? Tell everyone who'll listen about how you scored again with the easy city girl on the rebound?"

Hoping Nick had already left or that she might find a way to sneak by him, she turned toward the door. But Travis caught her arm before she took her first step, spinning her back around to face him. Up close, she saw what she'd missed in the dim patio lighting. His eyes were bleary, and judging by his gin-soaked breath, he'd had a lot more to drink than he should have.

"Let me go, Travis." His grip on her upper arm tightened at her words, and a tremor of fear shook her nerves.

"Better do what she says, Parker."

Relief rushed through Darcy as Nick stepped through the patio doors. Travis dropped his hand as he faced the other man, his body still blocking her from the exit. "Mind your own business, Pirelli. This is the second time you've butted in where you're not wanted."

"Funny. I'd say it's the second time you've refused to listen to the lady after she told you to back off. So this time I'm telling you. *Back off.*"

Travis stepped up to met the challenge, and Darcy took advantage of the opening as she slipped by him and headed for the patio doors...and Nick. His dark gaze searched her from head to toe, but before he could ask if she was unharmed, Travis charged. He landed a sucker punch Nick never saw coming, snapping his head back with the force of fist to flesh. Darcy barely had time to gasp before he caught his balance and took a shot of his own.

Travis reeled backward but caught Nick's arm at the last minute, and the two of them hit the ground amid a crash of tables and chairs and broken beer bottles. Horrified, Darcy lifted her gaze from the two men wrestling on the floor to the group of people who had quickly gathered on the patio.

She scanned the faces, searching for someone, anyone who might break up the fight, only to see Sam's grinning face as he took another swallow of his beer.

A shrill whistle pierced the night at the same time Nick hauled Travis to his feet, his fists tangled in the front of his shirt. "Okay, break it up, both of you," a blond-haired man insisted, shoving his way between the two men, "before the bartender ends up calling my dad."

The dry comment drew chuckles from the crowd and Darcy recognized Billy Cummings, the sheriff's son, as the man who'd broken up the fight.

Eyeing both Nick and Travis, Billy warned, "You know he'll throw your butts in a cell together until you shake hands or kill each other. I'm betting on the latter, so you might want to head home instead. Come on, everybody, back inside."

With a last glare at Nick, Travis stormed into the bar. Within minutes, Billy and Sam had waved everyone inside, leaving Nick and Darcy alone on the patio. Her fear gave way to fury, and rounding on him, she had half a mind to take up where Travis had left off.

"What were you thinking, Nick? Fighting in a bar? Not ten minutes after telling me how Carol is going to be digging up dirt, looking for anything she can use against you!"

Spotting an empty pitcher on a nearby table, Darcy picked it up and drained out the last of the ice through her still shaking fingers. She grabbed some napkins off a nearby table, wrapped the remaining ice inside and braced the slightly soggy cold compress against his quickly swelling eye.

Nick reached up to wrap his fingers around her wrist and gently pull her hand away. "I was defending the woman I love. A woman I'm beginning to think loves me, too, but is afraid to admit it." He swallowed. "I don't blame you for doubting me after the way I've acted. And I'll do whatever it takes, wait as long as I have to, to prove how much I love you and to show you that you can trust me again."

Trust me.

Darcy swallowed. She hadn't trusted him. Not with everything. Not with the truth that could cost him his daughter.

"You don't understand, Nick."

"So tell me. Whatever it is that's holding you back so we can move past it. I love you. Nothing you say will change that."

It was a vow she'd once hoped to hear from Aaron. A vow she still hoped to hear once she told Nick everything.

He righted two of the patio chairs and sat down in front of her, his hands still holdings hers as the whole story spilled out. How her mother wasn't just a single mother, but had been a teen mom, pregnant from an affair with a much older, very married businessman. How he'd ended the affair once Alanna became pregnant, wanting nothing to do with her or the baby she carried, interested only in saving his reputation and protecting his real family.

Saying the words left a hollow ache in her chest, but then Nick gave her hands a gentle squeeze. The caring and compassion in his gaze, so different from the shock and accusation she'd seen in Aaron's, filled that empty space and gave her the courage to go on.

"You're only the second person I've ever told the complete truth to. Aaron was the first."

"Your mama's-boy ex-fiancé?" Nick said.

Giving a watery laugh, Darcy nodded. "That's him. We were engaged, planning our wedding, and I had to tell him why I had no one from my father's side of the family to invite. He was shocked when I told him and accused me of purposely keeping my past a secret from him. And maybe I had. Maybe, deep down, I knew how he'd react."

"And that was when you broke up with him?"

"No, I was foolish enough to think we could still work things out. But then I overheard his mother tell him how marrying someone like me would only hold him back. How I was a liability. A dirty secret the opposition could use against Aaron to ruin everything he wanted in life. Standing outside the doorway, I waited for him to say all the things I thought he should say. That I was my own person, regardless of who my father was or wasn't. How my past wouldn't make any difference to the future we could have together. Mostly I waited for him to tell his mother he loved me for who I was. No matter what."

The rush of words slowed and then stopped, breaking down into pained and embarrassed silence. "When those words never came… That's when I broke up with Aaron."

"The man was an idiot, and his loss is my gain."

"I'm not so sure, Nick. I'm not so sure Aaron wasn't right. Marrying me—getting involved with me—was a risk he wasn't willing to take. It's a risk I can't let you take."

"Darcy—"

"I would have felt horrible if my past cost Aaron some election down the line, but that's nothing compared to how I'd feel if I cost you your daughter. She's the most important person in the world to you, Nick. You told me that from the start. She's your first priority, and I'm—"

"You're the woman I love."

But how long would that love last if the courts ruled in his ex-wife's favor? How long before he blamed her? The thought of watching the love in his eyes slowly dim and die made the small blossom of hope inside her wither away.

"But Maddie—"

"Clearville is her home, and it's where she wants to stay.

I'm going to fight to keep my daughter. And I want you at my side when I do. The three of us are stronger together."

The three of us...

"I don't know, Nick. I just…" Her words trailed off helplessly, miserably. She wanted to say yes with her whole heart, but Barbara Utley's accusations cut deeper now than they had months ago. The older woman had been so sure Darcy would cost her son his bright future.

How could she risk costing Nick his daughter?

He slid his hands out from beneath hers, and Darcy felt her heart break. Still caught in her own indecision, she watched helplessly as Nick stood and backed away. "I love you, Darcy. If that means letting you go and trusting that you'll come back to me, then that's what I'll do." The sound of laughter and music rose and fell as he opened the door to the bar and let it slowly close behind him.

Letting go... It was what she'd done her entire life. Protecting her heart, keeping people at a distance, making it easy to move on. But not this time. Her love for Nick wasn't something she could box up and store in a back bedroom, out of sight and out of mind. The love she felt was a part of her now—heart and soul and body.

And she couldn't lock it away any more than she could let him leave.

Pushing out of the chair, she raced back inside the bar and cut across the crowded dance floor. The press of bodies blocked her every step as she tried to slip through. A cowboy muttered an apology as she felt the cold splash of beer hit her foot, but she didn't stop moving. She had to find Nick.

The table where he'd been sitting with Sam and Debbie earlier was empty now, only a few bottles of beer and some peanut shells marking their place. Was she too late? Had he already left?

Cool night air hit her face as she left the heat of the restaurant and the smells of beer and barbecue behind. The restaurant's sign glowed overhead and a few lights illuminated the parking lot, giving off enough of a glow for Darcy to spot a familiar SUV and the man she loved waiting beside it.

Relief washed over his features as she raced across the uneven asphalt and into his arms. "I thought you were letting me go," she said, the words falling from her lips right along with the trembling tears from her eyes.

"I never said I'd let you go far." The tension in his body as he held her tightly betrayed his earlier certainty. "I know what I told you about our love being strong enough, but I swear, Darcy—"

"Never," she promised. "You'll never have to let me go again. I love you, Nick."

She'd moved to Clearville to find a place to call home, but in Nick's arms, she found so much more. Her heart, her home, her happiness. Her family.

Epilogue

Darcy promised herself she wouldn't cry at Sophia and Jake's wedding. It was a promise she kept even as the groomsmen stepped out from a side room in the small, sunlit chapel and took their places at the front of the church. Jake Cameron and the three Pirelli brothers all looked ruggedly handsome in their tuxedos. But it was Nick who stole her breath and refused to give it back as his dark gaze searched the guests and finally found Darcy toward the back of the church.

Her gaze may have become a little blurry when Maddie walked down the aisle, a huge smile on her face as she sprinkled rose petals along the satin runner. And Darcy's eyes definitely teared up as Jake kissed his beautiful bride. But only when Vince Pirelli led Sophia to the dance floor for the father-daughter dance did Darcy realize some promises were meant to be broken.

She gave a watery laugh as a snowy handkerchief appeared in front of her face. Snatching it from Nick's hand, she dabbed at her eyes and warned, "Don't you dare make fun of me."

"Wouldn't dream of it," he said solemnly despite the amusement in his brown eyes. "My mother made sure Sam, Drew and I all had those on hand, and I don't think it was because she thought the three of us were going to cry."

"Oh, no. Not manly men like you."

But then proving he wasn't a total tough guy, Nick gazed out at the dance floor beneath the tent lit with hundreds of twinkling lights. "Sophia looks happy, doesn't she?"

"She does."

Sophia's gown was simple yet elegant with an empire waist that draped over her rounded belly, cap sleeves and lace-covered bodice. Her short dark hair had been artfully curled and styled with tiny pink tea roses, and she hadn't stopped smiling since Jake slid the ring on her finger. Vince Pirelli, an older, mellower version of Nick, couldn't have looked any prouder, and the press of tears burned Darcy's eyes again.

"You okay?" Nick asked quietly.

"Your dad asked if I'd like him to give me away at our wedding," she said as she glanced up at him. "But you already knew that, didn't you?"

"He ran it by me first. He didn't want to step on any toes. I told him there weren't any toes to step on, just empty shoes that needed to be filled."

"What did he say?"

Nick grinned as he reached up to wipe another tear from beneath her eye. "That he always knew having big feet would come in handy someday."

Darcy wasn't the least bit surprised that she'd fallen for Nick's sometimes loud, always loving family as easily as she'd fallen for the serious, handsome vet. But she was still amazed and so thankful for the way they had opened their arms and welcomed her. The wedding was still two months away, but as far as the Pirellis were concerned, Darcy was already part of the family.

"Daddy!" An impatient Maddie raced over to Nick, her full skirt frothing at her ankles as she ran. "We need to dance."

"Not right now, sweetie," Nick started to protest.

"Yes, right now! Uncle Sam said this is the father-daughter dance, and I'm your daughter."

"You are but—" He glanced at Darcy as she squeezed his arm and nodded at the dance floor. "You're right, Maddie. This is a father-daughter dance, so what are we waiting for?"

With a look that promised he'd be back, Nick led the flower girl onto the dance floor beside Sophia and Vince. Darcy smiled as she watched the two of them together. The sight of her strong, solid fiancé wrapped around his daughter's little finger always went straight to the softest spot of her heart.

"Oh, look at that." Vanessa stepped beside her, sighing as the two generations of Pirelli fathers and daughters danced together. "How sweet."

"I think Nick was a little worried about butting into Sophia's father-daughter dance."

His mother shook her head. "Honestly, he should know better. We aren't exactly sticklers for formality and we're always butting into each other's lives."

"Uh-oh. Is that a warning?"

"Not a warning so much as a prelude of things to come." A soft smile curved the older woman's lips as she said, "But somehow I think you're up to it."

"Let's see—a family full of people who love and look

out for one another. I've pretty much been waiting for that my whole life."

"I'm sorry your mother couldn't be here to see you now and to enjoy the happiness you've found with my son."

"I am, too." Blinking back tears, she added, "But you know, it's funny. All her talk of moving back here… I don't think it was really something she wanted for herself as much as something she wanted for me. Like she knew everything I was looking for was right here, and she was pointing the way for me to find it. Does that sound crazy?"

"No, my dear. That sounds like a mother's love." Her knowing gaze followed Darcy's onto the dance floor where they watched as Nick swung a laughing Maddie around in a quick circle. "Something that you've gotten a taste of recently."

"Carol is Maddie's mother," she insisted. "I'm not trying to replace her."

"Of course not. But you'll find out that my granddaughter has a lot of love to give. There's plenty to go around," Vanessa remarked before drifting away to check on the caterers.

Darcy had more than enough love to embrace the little girl who would soon be her stepdaughter. And enough compassion to understand the insecurity behind the threats Carol had made. Once Darcy and Nick talked and came to the decision not to involve lawyers or to go through another custody battle, agreeing to let Maddie go to France for her regularly scheduled visit, Carol had confessed that was all she'd wanted in the first place.

Convincing Nick hadn't been easy until Darcy came up with the idea to combine the visit to Paris with their honeymoon. Maddie would stay with Carol, but Nick and Darcy would only be a short car ride away.

As excited as she was about their wedding and honeymoon, it was the life they'd start together afterward she most looked forward to. A life with the husband she loved and the home and family she'd found in this tiny town.

As the music changed on the dance floor, Jake claimed his bride and Maddie's grandfather swept her up into his arms, leaving Nick free to join his fiancée.

"What is that grin all about?" Darcy asked as he pulled her into his arms on the dance floor.

"You will never guess what Maddie wants to name the mama dog."

Though they were still looking for good homes for the puppies, Nick and Darcy had decided to keep the stray who'd wandered into Darcy's yard and brought Nick into her life. They'd gone through a dozen names so far with Maddie discarding each one.

"Hmm, I'm almost afraid to ask."

"Since all the puppies' names have to do with being born during a storm, she says we should name the mama dog Sunshine," he told her, his grin growing wider, "because it's stopped raining."

"I think that is just about perfect," Darcy agreed, the love in Nick's eyes promising a very bright future for them all.

* * * * *

Don't miss Sam's story, DADDY SAYS "I DO!"
the next installment in Stacy Connelly's new
Special Edition miniseries
THE PIRELLI BROTHERS,
on sale March 2013,
wherever Harlequin books are sold.

COMING NEXT MONTH
from Harlequin® Special Edition®
AVAILABLE JANUARY 22, 2012

#2239 A DATE WITH FORTUNE
The Fortunes of Texas: Southern Invasion
Susan Crosby

Michael Fortune comes to quaint Red Rock to persuade his cousins to come back to the family business in Atlanta. But when he meets Felicity, an adorable candy maker who owns a local chocolate shop, *she* may hold more weight than he's ready for.

#2240 A PERFECTLY IMPERFECT MATCH
Matchmaking Mamas
Marie Ferrarella

Jared Winterset throws his parents a celebratory party for their thirty-fifth wedding anniversary with the help of party planner and secret matchmaker Theresa Manetti. When he sees the sweet violinist Theresa strategically chose to entertain during the celebration, he winds up finding the woman *he* wants to marry.

#2241 THE COWBOY'S PREGNANT BRIDE
St. Valentine, Texas
Crystal Green

Cowboy Jared Colton has a dark past, and when he comes to St. Valentine to uncover some truth, he finds himself wanting to crack a different mystery...a pregnant bride who is running away from her own secrets.

#2242 THE MARRIAGE CAMPAIGN
Summer Sisters
Karen Templeton

Wes Phillips has proven his worthiness to win a seat in Congress, but does he have what it takes to win and heal Blythe Broussard's wounded heart?

#2243 HIS VALENTINE BRIDE
Rx for Love
Cindy Kirk

He loves her best friend. She, though helplessly in love with him, pretends to like *his* friend. Are they too far into a lie when he realizes that she's the one for him after all?

#2244 STILL THE ONE
Michelle Major

Lainey Morgan ran away with a hurtful secret the day of her wedding to Ethan Daniels. Now that she's beckoned to return and take care of her estranged mother, she's regretting her decision to leave Ethan at the altar. If she confronts him about the reason she fled, will he take her back?

You can find more information on upcoming Harlequin® titles, free excerpts and more at www.HarlequinInsideRomance.com.

HSECNM0113

REQUEST YOUR FREE BOOKS!

2 FREE NOVELS PLUS 2 FREE GIFTS!

◈ HARLEQUIN®

SPECIAL EDITION

Life, Love & Family

YES! Please send me 2 FREE Harlequin® Special Edition novels and my 2 FREE gifts (gifts are worth about $10). After receiving them, if I don't wish to receive any more books, I can return the shipping statement marked "cancel." If I don't cancel, I will receive 6 brand-new novels every month and be billed just $4.49 per book in the U.S. or $5.24 per book in Canada. That's a savings of at least 14% off the cover price! It's quite a bargain! Shipping and handling is just 50¢ per book in the U.S. and 75¢ per book in Canada.* I understand that accepting the 2 free books and gifts places me under no obligation to buy anything. I can always return a shipment and cancel at any time. Even if I never buy another book, the two free books and gifts are mine to keep forever.

235/335 HDN FVTV

Name	(PLEASE PRINT)

Address		Apt. #

City	State/Prov.	Zip/Postal Code

Signature (if under 18, a parent or guardian must sign)

Mail to the Harlequin® Reader Service:
IN U.S.A.: P.O. Box 1867, Buffalo, NY 14240-1867
IN CANADA: P.O. Box 609, Fort Erie, Ontario L2A 5X3

Want to try two free books from another line?
Call 1-800-873-8635 or visit www.ReaderService.com.

* Terms and prices subject to change without notice. Prices do not include applicable taxes. Sales tax applicable in N.Y. Canadian residents will be charged applicable taxes. Offer not valid in Quebec. This offer is limited to one order per household. Not valid for current subscribers to Harlequin Special Edition books. All orders subject to credit approval. Credit or debit balances in a customer's account(s) may be offset by any other outstanding balance owed by or to the customer. Please allow 4 to 6 weeks for delivery. Offer available while quantities last.

Your Privacy—The Harlequin® Reader Service is committed to protecting your privacy. Our Privacy Policy is available online at www.ReaderService.com or upon request from the Harlequin Reader Service.

We make a portion of our mailing list available to reputable third parties that offer products we believe may interest you. If you prefer that we not exchange your name with third parties, or if you wish to clarify or modify your communication preferences, please visit us at www.ReaderService.com/consumerchoice or write to us at Harlequin Reader Service Preference Service, P.O. Box 9062, Buffalo, NY 14269. Include your complete name and address.

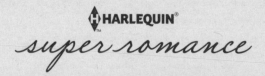

Wild for the Sheriff

by Kathleen O'Brien

On sale February 5

Dallas Garwood has always been the good guy, the one who does the right thing...except whenever he crosses paths with Rowena Wright. Now that she's back, things could get interesting for this small-town sheriff! Read on for an exciting excerpt from *Wild for the Sheriff* by Kathleen O'Brien.

Dallas Garwood had always known that sooner or later he'd open a door, turn a corner or look up from his desk and see Rowena Wright standing there.

It wasn't logical. It was simply an unshakable certainty that she wasn't gone for good, that one day she would return.

Not to see him, of course. He didn't kid himself that their brief interlude had been important to her. But she'd be back for Bell River—the ranch that was part of her.

Still, he hadn't thought today would be the day he'd face her across the threshold of her former home.

Or that she would look so gaunt. Her beauty was still there, but buried beneath some kind of haggard exhaustion. Her wild green eyes were circled with shadows, and her white shirt and jeans hung on her.

Something twisted in his chest, stealing his words. He'd never expected to feel pity for Rowena Wright.

She still knew how to look sardonic. She took him in, and he saw himself as she did, from the white-lightning scar dividing his right eyebrow to the shiny gold star pinned at his breast.

Three-tenths of a second. That was all it took to make him feel boring and overdressed, as if his uniform were as much a costume as his son Alec's cowboy hat.

"*Sheriff* Dallas Garwood." The crooked smile on her red lips was cryptic. "I should have known. Truly, I should have known."

"I didn't realize you'd come home," he said, wishing he didn't sound so stiff.

"Come *back*," she corrected him. "After all these years, it might be a bit of a stretch to call Bell River *home*."

"I see." He didn't really, but so what? He'd been her lover once, but never her friend.

The funny thing was, right now he'd give almost anything to change that and resurrect that long-ago connection.

Will Dallas and Rowena reconnect? Or will she skip town again with everything left unsaid? Find out in *Wild for the Sheriff* by Kathleen O'Brien, available February 2013 from Harlequin® Superromance®.

HSREXP0113